P9-DMH-525

# HURRICANE SEASON

# HURRICANE SEASON

Nicole Melleby

Algonquin Young Readers 2019

Published by
Algonquin Young Readers
an imprint of Algonquin Books of Chapel Hill
Post Office Box 2225
Chapel Hill, North Carolina 27515-2225

a division of
Workman Publishing
225 Varick Street
New York, New York 10014


Printed in the United States of America.
Published simultaneously in Canada by Thomas Allen & Son Limited.
Design by Carla Weise.

LIBRARY OF CONGRESS CATALOGING-IN-PUBLICATION DATA

Names: Melleby, Nicole, author.
Title: Hurricane season / Nicole Melleby.
Description: First edition. | Chapel Hill, North Carolina : Algonquin Young Readers, 2019. | Summary: Eleven-year-old Fig enrolls in an art class to better understand her father, a composer and pianist whose mental illness she tries to conceal from classmates, neighbors, and social services.
Identifiers: LCCN 2018033589 | ISBN 9781616209063 (hardcover : alk. paper)
Subjects: | CYAC: Manic-depressive illness—Fiction. | Musicians—Fiction. | Fathers and daughters—Fiction.
Classification: LCC PZ7.1.M46934 Hu 2019 | DDC [Fic]—dc23
LC record available at https://lccn.loc.gov/2018033589

10 9 8 7 6 5 4 3 2 1
First Edition

To Donna.
I don't think it's hyperbole to say
"for everything."

# PART ONE

## September

*The beginning is perhaps more*
*difficult than anything else,*
*but keep heart,*
*it will turn out all right.*

—Vincent van Gogh to his brother Theo,
January 1873

# THE YELLOW HOUSE

IT ALL STARTED THE DAY FIG NOTICED THE SOLD addition to the sign on her neighbor's lawn as she left for school.

She sat at her desk in art class with her chin resting on her hands as her art teacher asked Danny Carter to pass out large, clean white sheets of paper. It was a warm day for September, and Fig kept her eyes focused out the classroom window at the bright blue sky as the class ticked by. Haley Flores was handing out paper plates, and Miss Williams was walking around the room, asking everyone to pick the three colors of paint they wanted to start with.

Ava Washington was playing with her cell phone under her desk, and Madison Sherman leaned over to ask, "Would it be stupid to say I wanted green paint?"

Sixth-grade business as usual.

Danny handed Fig a sheet of paper. "You could ask for blue and yellow instead," he said to Madison. "You shouldn't waste your pick on green."

That was when the classroom door flew open and everyone turned with wide excited eyes to see what the disruption was. The school year had barely started, but any interruption from the routine of lectures and paint was a welcome one.

But the distraction was anything but welcome for Fig when she saw that it was her dad standing in the doorway. "Fig?" His voice was wobbly and small.

Everyone turned away from him to look, instead, at her.

Fig's dad shuffled his feet as he entered the classroom, looking for her and bumping into one of the desks. He knocked over the entire box of paintbrushes in the process, causing Miss Williams to spill the jar of blue paint all over her hand. Fig stood, trying to get her dad's attention as Danny began picking up the brushes, and Miss Williams said calmly, "Can I help you, Mr. Arnold? Is everything okay?"

Miss Williams gently grasped his arm with her now-blue fingers. Startled, he looked at her. "Is Fig here?" he asked. "I'm . . . I'm looking for Fig. I didn't know where she . . . They said she was . . ."

"Right here," Fig whispered. "I'm right here, Dad."

His eyes were unfocused as they settled on her. It was a look Fig was familiar with, one she hated. One she didn't want her classmates to see. "Fig. Come on, let's go." He reached for her hand as he stepped toward her, grabbing onto it a little too tightly.

She was about to follow him because she knew he needed her, but Miss Williams grasped his arm, again. "Mr. Arnold, why don't we step out in the hallway for a moment."

"I need . . . Look, I just need my kid." His voice started nearing the desperate twinge Fig hated to hear.

Fig knew how to take care of her dad at home, but she had a hard time focusing on him now. All around her, her classmates were watching and whispering. Ava had her phone right there on her desk, and Fig knew how much she liked to take pictures. Haley was giggling with Madison, and Danny was still standing in the center of the room, too close to Fig's dad, gripping the tin of paint-brushes tightly and staring.

"Fig, please," her dad said, and Fig knew she would go with him.

But then Miss Williams held out her hand. "How about the three of us just go into the hall for a moment, okay, Mr. Arnold? Me, you, and Fig."

Fig looked up into Miss Williams's eyes, soft and kind and understanding. When Fig took Miss Williams's paint-covered fingers and her dad quickly grabbed for Fig's other hand, she felt like she had betrayed him. The whispers around Fig grew louder, and Miss Williams continued to hold her ground, continued to say her dad's name.

"Mr. Arnold. Come with me, Mr. Arnold. Just come with me to the hallway."

A week later, Fig could still hear her father's panicked voice in her head, could see the hurt in his eyes. She was also discovering more and more repercussions of that moment, including the lady from Child Protection and Permanency who—and not for the first time—came knocking on their door.

Fig, try as she did, couldn't stop thinking about CP&P, which was New Jersey's department of social services—or how this time they would be keeping a close eye on her and her dad. Nor could she stop thinking about how her classmates might figure out how poorly his mind worked and how, because of that, CP&P could take him away from her. They were both—CP&P and her classmates—starting to ask a lot of questions. She leaned against the back of the living room couch, looking out the window at the small yellow house across the street, where her neighbor Ms. Minkle was carrying boxes outside.

Ms. Minkle was moving, and Fig had to blink back tears watching her. Ms. Minkle was a good neighbor. She kept to herself. Sometimes she'd wave, but she never made small talk, and every so often her boyfriend even brought in their garbage cans when Fig's dad forgot and the wind blew the bins and the garbage all over the road.

Most important, Ms. Minkle never called anyone about her strange neighbors across the street, unlike Fig's school and Miss Williams.

Fig watched from the window as Ms. Minkle packed her things into her bright blue car, while the voices from the weather broadcast on TV mingled with the sounds of Fig's dad's slightly out-of-tune piano being tinkered into submission behind her.

All of which added to the knot in Fig's stomach.

"Is it a hurricane yet?" Her dad's voice was a more welcome sound than his piano. She loved that she could still hear traces of his old east London accent that didn't belong anywhere near their home in New Jersey. "I would like a hurricane."

"Still a tropical storm," Fig responded. She did *not* want a hurricane. "It won't become a hurricane. It's not strong enough, and it'll make landfall soon."

"I love the sounds of a good storm." He climbed out from under his small wooden upright piano, leaving it open with its insides exposed. It always fascinated Fig how easily her dad understood the inner workings of a piano when neither of them understood the inner workings of him.

Fig reached a hand up to brush it through her knotty, messy hair. The last thing she needed was another reason to stand out in school. She really wanted to fade back into the background. It had been a long, long week of questions and gossip. "Will you braid my hair?"

Her dad rarely refused her when he was well, and he slid to one side of the piano bench and patted the spot in front of him for Fig to settle between his knees, which she did easily. She was small for her age, but she supposed he was, too. She never worked up the nerve to ask how tall her mother was—she had been gone since the day after Fig was born—but she could only assume she got her height from him. She handed him her hairbrush, and he ran his fingers through her bed-mussed black hair.

Fig may not have appreciated his musical skill, but she did appreciate his calloused piano-playing fingers as he scratched softly at her scalp with his cut-too-short nails. She'd be lying if she said he was good at braiding hair, but he was better at it than she, and he always tried hard, and, really, she had no better option. Truth be told, she could understand why her mother didn't stay; her dad was a difficult man to live with.

What she couldn't understand, however, was how her mother could leave *her*, little and pink and new, and Fig wondered what would have been different this past week if she hadn't. It took a special sort of person to live with and love her father, and Fig considered herself mighty special, but she was still the one left to face her classmates.

"Everyone at school has a smartphone, you know," she said, flipping her subpar phone open and closed for effect.

"How lovely for them," her dad said, and finished twisting the band at the end of her long braid. "All done."

"Dad, I'm literally the only sixth grader without one," Fig tried again. "This thing is embarrassing." She flipped it open and closed again, holding it up like some sort of ancient artifact.

"Embarrassment builds character."

"Not in middle school! It builds miserable children! Dad, you don't understand."

He leaned forward to press his forehead against hers, closing his eyes and humming along to a tune only he could hear, one that was trapped in his head and leaking out of him the way songs often did.

The humming slowly came to a stop, the song in his head ending. His eyes met hers as he softly admitted, "A smartphone would be one more bill to stress over."

That she did understand. And, considering all that was happening, it made her feel guilty.

He kissed her forehead, the stubble on his face scratching a bit, and sat back up. Fig made a face. He always forgot to shave when his mind was elsewhere. "When was the last time you shaved?"

Her dad gave her a sheepish grin, his eyes wrinkling at the corners. "I'll do it later."

She sighed and popped off the bench to go and grab her backpack and shoes strewn by the front door.

"Don't I get a kiss?" her dad called after her.

She shook her head. "Not until you shave!"

He ran a hand over his too-scratchy-for-kisses stubble. Fig was starting to notice more gray in the light brown color of it lately. "Hold back a second, Fig."

"I'm going to miss my bus."

He didn't say anything for a moment, and Fig hovered by the door. The knot in her stomach grew tighter.

"Everything is going to be okay," he finally said. "I just . . . I want you to know that when they come back . . . it's going to be okay."

She glanced past him to the calendar they hung on the wall, right above his piano. It was where they wrote down all of Fig's school things, all their appointments, all the notes needed so her dad wouldn't forget or be confused about any of it. It was the first week of September. In three months, on November 30, written in heavy ink and circled twice in the little square space on that date, was their newly scheduled follow-up CP&P visit. It was also the very last day of hurricane season.

Fig wanted to tell her dad that she believed him, that everything between now and then would be okay.

She nodded instead.

"I love you, darling."

"Double it," Fig said as she opened the front door, stepping into the humidity that still clung to the early fall air.

"Love you, love you!" he called back.

Her bus stop was at the end of the street, past four more houses that looked identical to hers, all in various stages of repair. Their own white wooden door was splintered at the knob. Fig stood with three other kids who were older and taller and louder than she was. They all stopped talking when she got on line, and she looked down at her shoes, pretending the silence was just coincidence, even though she knew it wasn't. Their school was small, and news spread fast, and the kids from her neighborhood already knew more than the rest of her classmates. The school bus pulled up with creaks and clanks, the door sliding open with a screech that Fig hated.

Before the doors closed behind her, she watched as Ms. Minkle drove away, and she was sad all over again. She could only hope that whoever moved in to the yellow house next would be just as quick to turn a blind eye on her dad.

# 2

# SELF-PORTRAIT

SUBJECTS FIG WAS GOOD AT: MATH AND SCIENCE AND the other wonderful letters of STEM. Subjects Fig was not good at: anything related to art.

At eleven years old, Fig already knew a lot about budgets and bank accounts and checkbooks and credit cards. She knew what bills she and her dad had to pay, and how much money they needed to pay them. She may still have had a lot to learn about algebra, but she was bright enough to know how to make sure she and her dad had enough money to get on while still having some left over to buy her favorite cereal, and his favorite tea—neither of which were the store brand.

Her dad was the artist, and while he always claimed that musicians used the same side of the brain as mathematicians, Fig wasn't so sure. Math she understood. Art and music, the whole language that her dad spoke and played and hummed, made very little sense to her.

Fig hated that. She hated that the one clear thing in her dad's world was the one thing she couldn't make sense of. Which is why, to the shock of her school counselor, she chose art instead of science lab as her elective.

But now, as she and her classmates sat in art class with instructions to sketch a piece that each of them would be painting in a few weeks, the only thing she wanted was for Miss Williams not to come anywhere near her. As everyone else scratched away, the sounds of pencils on paper mingling with the low murmurs of sixth-grade gossip and flirting, Fig stared at her blank sketchpad at a complete loss and utterly distraught over it.

It didn't help matters that Jeremy Ng sat next to her, smelling like a bag of Doritos (the red-bag nacho-cheese kind, not the blue-bag cool-ranch kind). Ava Washington, followed by all her friends, filled out the desks on the other side. Ava always had her long hair in braids that were much neater and tighter than any Fig ever wore, and most of the noise in the art room came from her and her friends. That noise engulfed Fig, who was close enough to *almost* pretend she was a part of it as they planned an after-school trip to Starbucks, even though they hadn't actually invited her anywhere all week.

Madison Sherman, from her usual spot next to Ava, caught Fig's gaze. "You can come if you want," she said.

Fig looked at their faces. The other girls didn't object, but they didn't exactly agree, either. None of them made eye contact with her, but they all exchanged glances with one another. "Really?" Fig asked.

Madison nodded, her short frizzy hair bouncing with her. No one else said anything. Still, not one of them objected. "Okay," Fig said.

That was all it took for Haley Flores to change the subject, and for the rest of them to turn away from Fig and focus again on one another. Fig sighed and stared back down at her blank piece of paper.

"Do you know what you're going to draw yet?"

Fig frowned as she turned to find Danny Carter sitting next to her. He had swapped seats with Jeremy, and Fig looked down at his paper, which was covered with pencil smudges and eraser bits. "I keep changing my mind," he said, sweeping his floppy blond bangs to the side of his head the way that all boys his age with long hair seemed to do. He had a gap between his two front teeth that gave his words a whistling sound as he spoke.

"Uh, no. I don't know yet," Fig said. She hadn't even picked up her pencil.

Danny pressed his lips into a thin line and gave Fig a determined nod. "You'll figure it out," he said.

"Having a hard time deciding what to draw?" Miss Williams asked, coming up behind Fig. Miss Williams smiled her wide smile full of large straight teeth, which Fig used to love but now made her stomach hurt.

Fig shrugged.

"Oh, come on." Miss Williams gently bumped her shoulder into Fig's. "We're going to display these at the Fall Festival. Don't you want to have something for your family to come and see?"

Fig didn't respond. It didn't matter to her what hung in the showcase. Her dad was all she had, and how could she ask him to come back to the school, in front of her classmates, where he could do something worse, where he could be laughed at, where *she* could be laughed at, where it could all get messed up again?

Miss Williams's smile fell, and for a moment Fig felt good about that. Fig thought she liked Miss Williams. She thought she liked that Miss Williams's hair was short and brushed up against Fig's cheek when she leaned over to see Fig's papers. She thought she liked that Miss Williams didn't ever tell Fig she was bad at art, and that

Miss Williams might be able to open up the world of art that Fig's dad lived in and that Fig wanted to understand.

But Miss Williams was the one who had called CP&P.

"Maybe you need some inspiration," Miss Williams suddenly said. "Wait right here."

Fig watched as Miss Williams crossed the room to the bookshelf behind her desk and pulled out the biggest hardcover book on it. When she crossed back and dropped it onto Fig's desk with a heavy thud, Fig's eyes opened wide.

Danny's did, too. "Oh, cool!" he said.

Fig didn't think it was all that cool. "You're giving me more work?"

Miss Williams laughed. "Just flip through it when you can. It's a book of artists, all different kinds. Take it home. We won't be painting for a couple weeks yet. You have time to figure it out."

Fig was pretty sure the book wouldn't even fit in her backpack, but she was polite about it anyway. "Thank you."

"Maybe seeing and understanding the way other artists think will help."

Fig's eyes shot up to meet Miss Williams's—they were big and gentle in the same way they had been when Fig's dad showed up in class—and the knot in Fig's stomach tightened. She looked back down at the book on her desk, turning through the pages. Actually, this could be exactly what she needed.

"And Fig . . ." Miss Williams's voice grew quieter as she bent down closer to Fig, but Fig could tell Danny was still listening. "I know things are difficult right now. I want you to know that I'm here if you need anything. You just come and ask."

Fig knew she wouldn't be asking. She didn't need Miss Williams's help. She needed Miss Williams to understand that she made a mistake, that she was the reason things were difficult—that Fig was fine and didn't need her, or CP&P, or anyone but her dad.

Fig didn't respond. Miss Williams took the hint and, with a gentle squeeze to Fig's shoulder, moved on to Danny. Fig kept her eyes on the art book, tracing the swirling pattern of the sky on the cover.

If Fig could understand how her dad thought, maybe she could help him. Maybe she could make all the problems she caused go away.

Fig carried that heavy book around the rest of the day.

Fig didn't have the money for a Frappuccino, but she sat with Ava, Madison, and Haley as the three of them drank their own whipped-cream-topped drinks at the Starbucks near school. She called her dad from the bathroom so that the other girls didn't see her flip phone and left a message to let him know why she would be home late.

"Haley, can your mom drive me home?" Fig asked when she sat down again.

Haley nodded and pulled out her smartphone. "Yeah, I'll text and make sure."

"Your dad can't drive, right?" Ava said, her mouth full of mocha. "How'd he even get to school last week, then?"

Fig felt warm as the girls all looked at her. "He can, he just doesn't really."

"Why?" Ava asked, unbraiding and twirling the tips of her hair that her mom probably spent careful time on that morning.

"He doesn't feel good sometimes."

"What did he want you for so badly the other day, anyway?"

Starbucks was getting more and more crowded as all the schools in the area were being dismissed. The line was nearly out the door, filled with public school students like Fig and ones in uniforms from the Catholic school up the street. It was loud, and full, and Fig took off her sweater because it was getting too warm. "He just needed to see me."

Madison laughed. "It was a little weird, don't you think so?"

Fig *didn't* think so, but she didn't want to tell them that. She didn't want them to know any more than they already thought they did. She wanted to let them think her dad was weird. It was much better than thinking he was crazy.

The real story was: Her dad was a brilliant composer, once. He sold music all over England, and Europe, and then the United States. He moved to New York City and bought a studio apartment with a giant window that gave him a view that he said "people would die to see." No one in their town of Keansburg knew any of this, and even Fig found it difficult to believe. It seemed like a part of him that barely existed, just like the accent he hardly kept from a home he no longer had a connection to. The last piece of real music he wrote was sitting in the drawer of his desk. It was called "Finola," which was Fig's real name, and it was written the week she was born. He hadn't been able to finish, let alone sell, any music since.

(Fig tried not to wonder if it was her fault—if having her made the music go away. If her dad went looking for the music in the middle of storms or if it got trapped in his head because he had Fig, and her mom had left, and things got so much harder.)

What the neighbors heard—and complained about—were his halfhearted attempts to try to create something from his piano, jotting notes on old pieces of sheet music that he wrote on and whited out and scribbled on over and over again—trying to find something Fig was almost certain he had lost, even though she was uncertain when he had lost it. What they heard was his ranting and raving as students showed up at their door from NYU and other schools—students who had heard the man was bonkers but brilliant, students who needed that extra push, willing to withstand anything to get it. Students, coming fewer and farther between as the years went on, who were willing to take a chance on the once-renowned Tim Arnold.

The neighbors knew Fig's dad would sometimes not leave the house for days, and when he finally did, he would walk the streets of their town, to the boardwalk, to the sand of the beach and the edge of the ocean, letting the water lap at his feet as he stood there until Fig or a policeman could convince him to go home.

What the neighbors knew was that last year, in the middle of the biggest hurricane Jersey had seen in decades (the only one Fig could even remember), sirens and police lights went up and down the neighboring streets while a police cruiser sat outside Fig's house and a policeman sat inside with Fig, until they found her dad and brought him home. He ended up sick for two weeks, and the only thing he had to say to her about the whole ordeal was, "I wanted to hear the music, love."

But Fig's friends from school didn't know any of it. Nor did she want them to. "Yeah. My dad's just weird sometimes," she said, and she felt sick to her stomach.

It was enough for them to go back to talking about Madison's crush on Mikey Ramirez, and drinking their Frappuccinos, and doing all the things that Fig wished she could also so easily do with them.

Fig hoisted Miss Williams's heavy art book high on her hip as she thanked Haley's mom for the ride home. She was waving goodbye to Haley, watching them pull out of the driveway, when she caught sight of an unfamiliar truck. It sat across the street—where Ms. Minkle's bright blue car used to be—and it was big and gray and rusty. A man Fig had never seen before swung open the door of Ms. Minkle's yellow house, which had always been squeaky and somewhat off its hinges, and made his way toward the truck, grabbing a duffel bag from the back and swinging it over his shoulder.

Fig sighed. She thought they would have more time between neighbors.

He was tall and stood straight, even with the large and heavy-looking duffel bag hanging on one of his broad shoulders. His hair was cut short, neat and gray on his head, and he wore a Michigan State sweatshirt. He looked older than her dad but also much healthier.

He stopped when he saw her standing there, staring at him from across the street. He shifted the duffel bag to his other shoulder and lifted his hand in a small wave.

Fig didn't wave back at him. Her neighbors knew much more than her friends, but they didn't know everything. They didn't know the man who braided her hair and stayed with her until she fell asleep on the nights when she couldn't. They didn't know the man who once stayed up all night watching YouTube videos of how to sew so he could help make her a *Tangled* Halloween costume. This new one, right now, knew nothing. She wanted to keep it that way.

The man awkwardly lowered his hand and turned, shutting the back of the truck with an echoing slam. Fig made her way up the walkway but stopped when she reached the front door, turning back around to look at her new neighbor once more, watching as he headed up the driveway and into his new little yellow house.

Fig dropped the art book inside the door as soon as she walked into her house. She kicked off her shoes and abandoned her backpack in the same place, and set off to find her dad. "Dad? I'm home! Did you write anything today?"

The answer was always a long story that really meant "no" but entertained her anyway. Fig was almost certain he made every single detail up just to keep her from worrying. One day the week before, he claimed he spent over two hours writing what he knew was going to be the best piece of music ever written. Only, when he finally played it all back and listened to it, he realized it was actually just a fancy version of "Happy Birthday." Fig laughed but didn't believe a word of it. She liked to think he was still much better than that.

He wasn't at his piano, or in the bedroom that he treated more like a study than an actual bedroom. "Dad?"

Fig padded barefoot through the hallway and the kitchen before she realized she had walked right by him. She found him sound asleep on the couch, curled into the cushions and into himself, his hands wrapped tightly around a throw pillow.

This wasn't particularly unusual. It didn't happen often, but Fig didn't like it when it did. On days like this one he could sleep for hours—he had probably been sleeping through most of the day—and she doubted he even got her message that she would be late. She used to try to wake him but had learned there was no point. He would move when he was ready, if he would be at all. She kissed his forehead (he still hadn't shaved, so he was lucky he even got that) and left the room only for as long as it took to retrieve her backpack. She sat crisscross on the floor in front of him and moved aside his half-drunk teacup to do her homework at the coffee table.

The TV was tuned to the Weather Channel, showing a radar map of Tropical Storm Diane as it made its way toward the coast. Fig reached for the remote, her finger hovering over the power button as the weather people discussed barometric pressure and wind speeds and all the things that should keep any sane person away from standing out in the middle of a major storm.

Fig turned off the TV. Hurricane season lasted from the beginning of June until the end of November. They had made it three months without one. They needed to make it three more.

She pulled open her dad's laptop and loaded Netflix. Madison's username and password were auto-filled from early in the school year when she came over to work on a project and they watched Netflix instead. The thought made Fig's stomach drop, and she looked back at her dad, who was still sound asleep. She didn't know when it'd be okay to invite Madison—or anybody—to her house again.

Fig got lost in a show and her algebra homework, and her stomach had only begun growling when her dad finally shifted and turned over behind her. She leaned back into the couch and smiled when he opened his eyes to look at her.

"Hello, darling."

"Hi."

He blinked, and just like she noticed the growing gray in his stubble, she now noticed the soft gray of his eyelashes. "Have you been home long?"

"Not too long." It wasn't that much of a lie.

Her dad closed his eyes again and exhaled heavily before looking at her once more. "I was supposed to give James a lesson today."

"It's okay."

"It's really not."

Financial security was important. The CP&P lady had mentioned that.

"I changed my mind," Fig said. Another white lie. "I don't need a smartphone."

Her father slowly lifted himself upright, shifting aside to create space. "Sit with me for a bit?"

Fig climbed onto the couch and into his arms. Sometimes she wondered about the day when she would be too old for this, or a possible future where it could be taken away, but she shook those thoughts out of her mind. She rested her head against her dad's shoulder, trying just to enjoy the moment.

He pressed his lips to her hair, murmuring, "Once I sell a song, I'll buy you that phone. I promise. I'm sorry."

She wouldn't hold him to a promise she knew he couldn't keep. "Are you working on something?"

"Got half a piece done today, actually. And started another. But that was early on, and I must have wiped myself out."

"Can I hear them?"

"Maybe soon. Once they're finished." He closed his eyes and held her tight. "How was your day?"

"Fine. We have a new neighbor. And Miss Williams lent me an art book to help with a project we have."

"Art! How exciting."

"They're going to display the finished projects at the Fall Festival." The words left her mouth without a thought. She wasn't sure why she was telling him this.

His breathing was starting to even out, and he kept his eyes closed. "That sounds nice."

"It's right before Thanksgiving." Right before the end of hurricane season. Right before the CP&P follow-up.

When she spoke again, it was a whisper. "Will you come?"

"Hmm?"

She inhaled deeply to give herself the time to get a handle on her nerves. Because she wanted him there. She wanted her classmates and Miss Williams and everyone to see that everything was okay. That what they saw wasn't who her dad was. That he wasn't what they thought he was. "Please will you come to the Fall Festival?"

His smile was slow and lazy. "Anything for you, love."

Within seconds, he was asleep.

# A Pair of Shoes

Some days, no one would have been able to tell that Fig's dad spent other days entirely in bed. Today was one of those, and Fig covered her head with her pillow and groaned as he entered her bedroom and immediately flipped on the light, something he was well aware she hated.

"It's Saturday!" came her pillow-muffled response to the ordeal.

"It's gorgeous out, Fig, and I'm feeling a walk. Let's go to the beach," he said. "There's only so many more nice days left. Let's not let them go to waste."

So with groggy eyes and one of her dad's old semi-clean Royal Academy of Music shirts thrown over her bathing suit, Fig left her bedroom and walked over to the calendar hung by the piano. She crossed off yesterday's date—one day closer to November. She put the pen down and turned to find her dad watching her, his hands fidgeting against his thighs.

"Ready to go?" he asked, his eyes avoiding the calendar.

She followed him along their street and down the three blocks it took to get to the boardwalk. Her short legs had to do a lot of work to keep up with his (which were also short but moved much more quickly).

The busy end of the boardwalk—the part with the game booths and Bev & Wally's Arcade and Timoney's Pizzeria, and funnel cakes and fried Oreos and amusement park rides—was still crowded, even if most of the shops had closed at the end of the summer. The beach itself was more than half filled with towels and beach chairs and umbrellas, packed with all the locals who wanted to enjoy the last licks of the warm sun and the feel of salt water in the air before the season changed. Especially since lately the weather went from summer to winter and right back again, fall and spring taking a back burner to climate change.

But these were the days the locals lived for, the ones that were still beach days after tourist season, when they got to enjoy the place they called home.

Fig's dad, even if he still called London home, was one of those locals. The difference was that he would still go to the beach even when the locals stopped. He so loved looking at the ocean.

Which was why they were there.

Besides a piano bench, this was her dad's favorite place to be: shoes discarded in the sand, toes in the lapping waves of the ocean, staring out at all that blue—the dark blue of the water, the pale blue of the sky. Not moving, not speaking, just . . . looking. At what, Fig never really knew. She knew he liked the sky better on cloudy days, on stormy ones, when it swirled with dark angry colors, the white-capped waves swelling and sloshing, the mist from the rain and the salt from the sea on his face. She knew he liked to hum, his fingers tapping against his legs as he played tunes only he could hear. He was always filled with melodies that would probably never make it to paper, stuck in his head with all the things Fig wished she could hear and know and reach but couldn't.

Her dad watched the ocean, and Fig watched him, hoping something he might say or hum or confide in her would unlock the part of his mind that they both knew was broken, that Fig desperately wanted to understand. The part of him they never talked about, that made him want to stand in the middle of a storm last year and put them on CP&P's radar before this new mess even started—and made Fig count down to the end of hurricane season, hoping they wouldn't get one this year, or next year, or for a very, very long time.

"Beautiful, isn't it?" he said. "Like a work of art."

Fig opened her mouth to say, *Tell me what you see, tell me about art and music so I can do well in art class, and understand your mind, and then everything will be okay.*

But she was interrupted by someone shouting, "Fig! Over here!"

She turned and spotted Madison waving at her, not even ten feet away, sharing a blanket with Ava and Haley. They were lying out, wearing bikinis (even if the day was a little too breezy) and playing music from a small Bluetooth speaker, trying to keep their tans as long as they could into the school year.

Fig wanted to go sit and tan with them, but then her dad started to untie his shoes. She quickly grabbed his arm, stopping him. "What're you doing?"

"Just going to put my feet in the water."

"No, Dad. It's too cold."

He took his shoes off anyway, and walked to the edge of the beach, the waves lapping at his toes. Fig stood behind him, looking back and forth between him and her friends. They were watching. And they were giggling.

(Were they giggling at her? At him?)

She reached again for his hand, tugging on it, wanting to get them both out of Ava's and Madison's and Haley's and everyone's eyesight. "It's chilly here, Dad. I want to go back by the boardwalk."

"One moment, love."

She tugged harder. He would stand there forever if she let him, if there weren't policemen who patrolled the beaches at night to send him home. "Please. I'm hungry. Let's get pizza." He still didn't move, and she reached to grasp his elbow because she was all too aware that very little separated them from the cameras on Madison's and Ava's and Haley's phones. "I'm hungry, Dad."

He blinked but finally turned away from the water to look at Fig instead.

"Right," he said, running a hand over his unshaven face. "Pizza, then?"

As they walked back up the beach to the boardwalk, her dad kept turning to look at the ocean. Fig kept looking, too, hoping that maybe something out there would stand out, something in that view would make sense, but she saw nothing but the Atlantic. All the while the girls from her class lay on their blanket, listening to their music and forgetting that Fig was even there at all.

With pizza slices on grease-stained paper plates in their hands, Fig and her dad walked off the boardwalk toward home. Fig had pizza juice dripping down her chin, and she reached to steal the napkins her dad had grabbed and shoved in his pocket.

Turning the corner off the boardwalk and onto their street, Fig squinted as she recognized their new neighbor. He was jogging toward them, wearing gym shorts and sneakers. Fig jutted out her chin. "That's our new neighbor," she informed her dad.

Her dad made a noise that sounded like a question, but he was taking a huge bite out of his pizza—with hot cheese pulling off in strings as he tried to chew—so she didn't catch a word of it.

The new occupant of the yellow house wasn't a slouch; he was quickly approaching them. Fig heard her dad swallow loudly, and she knew it was coming before she could beg him not to. Once their neighbor was close enough, her dad yelled "Oi!" and immediately got his attention.

Their neighbor slowed to a stop, his eyebrows raised, as he pulled an earbud out of one ear. “Hey?” He said it like a question.

Fig wanted to go home. Their neighbors were cruel to her dad. This one was new—and here they were, greasy messes with half-eaten pizza and wind-wild hair from a couple of hours spent walking the beach and staring at the ocean, and who knew what one more bad phone call to CP&P could do.

Her dad didn’t seem to share her concerns. “Apparently you’re our new neighbor. You’re across the street, in the yellow house?” he asked, and their new neighbor nodded. “Thought I’d introduce myself, though I suppose better neighbors would have brought over a casserole. I’m Tim Arnold. This is my daughter, Fig.”

“Finola,” Fig said, before he could ask. “Fig’s a nickname.”

“Mark Finzi,” he said, introducing himself and holding out his hand to Fig’s dad.

They shook hands, and Fig couldn’t help but compare the two. Mark looked as sturdy as a pillar; he seemed strong enough to hold a foundation up. He had a full head of gray hair and worry lines along his face, but she wouldn’t look at him and dare to call him old. Her dad, on the other hand, always slouched to the point of looking crooked, and no matter how much he slept, he always had bags under his eyes. He wasn't out of shape, but it wasn't like he worked out, either. His hair also had a habit of sticking out however it pleased, and the salty beach air didn't exactly help tame it.

"*Finzi*. Like the composer," her dad said, and Fig suffered to keep from rolling her eyes. She held her breath and prayed the conversation would move quickly.

"Ah, I wouldn't know," Mark replied.

"Gerald Finzi—"

"Dad, he doesn't know," Fig interrupted, then addressed Mark, smiling and trying to get him to understand. "He does this, he can't help it. Music was his life once—"

"And then I had Fig."

Fig paused, taking a moment to keep the smile on her face. She knew her dad didn't mean it like that, but still. She sometimes couldn't help thinking she took that part of him away. "And then he had me. But he forgets that not everyone cares."

Mark smiled, and his face looked gentler. Not younger, exactly, but fuzzier and softer around the edges. "Not that I don't care. Just not really a music guy."

"And here we were getting on so well," Fig's dad said. "Well, nice meeting you. Sorry we aren't the casserole type."

"Dad . . ."

Mark kept smiling. "I'll see you two around, then."

He gave them both a wave as he put the earbud back in and began jogging. Fig sighed in relief. As far as first impressions go, this was possibly one of her dad's finest.

"He seems nice," her dad said as they watched Mark go.

At home, as her dad attempted to get the sand off his feet before going inside ("I swear this sand is like glue!"), Fig decided to crack open the large, heavy art book Miss Williams had lent her.

She was familiar with some of the paintings she saw as she flipped through the pages. She recognized the work of Picasso, had seen a couple of Salvador Dalí's paintings before. She knew Edvard Munch's *The Scream*, knew Da Vinci's *Mona Lisa*, knew Van Gogh's *Starry Night*.

"Homework on a Saturday?" her dad commented as he entered the living room with newly donned socks on his feet.

"Art project I told you about."

"Ah. See anything you like?"

"This book is mostly men," Fig said, pulling a face. "But look. This one kind of looks like you." She held open the book to a page of one of Vincent van Gogh's self-portraits.

He snorted. "I'm not ginger."

"The rest of it," Fig said. "Especially when you don't shave."

"I'll shave later."

"Thank you."

"Maybe get one of those straw hats, too."

Her dad plopped onto the couch and turned on the Weather Channel. Fig continued to flip through the Van Gogh section of the art book, then pushed it to the side and pulled over her dad's laptop to do a Google image search to look at more. She didn't understand all of his work—particularly what was so fascinating about a bowl of fruit or a chair—but she thought Van Gogh's landscapes were pretty. And his yellow house reminded her of Ms. Minkle—and now Mark—across the street.

She thought about the self-portrait, Van Gogh's art, and about the last piece of music her dad finished—the one titled "Finola" that he kept in his desk. He named that song for her, and sometimes, when he was okay, she could convince him to play parts of it. Sometimes her dad couldn't find the words for his thoughts; sometimes they got lost or trapped in his head. Those times, he'd play her song, and Fig would know—she would *know*—that even on his worst days, he loved her more than everything.

Those days, she really did believe things would be okay.

Fig liked that Van Gogh's portrait reminded her of her dad the way her dad's music sometimes reminded him of her.

She closed the heavy art book.

Maybe Vincent van Gogh would be a good place to start.

# TREE ROOTS

Fig was hesitant as she approached Miss Williams's desk. She didn't know how to act. Miss Williams saw past her dad's confusion to what was really going on. She knew too much that Fig didn't want her to know. She didn't want to give Miss Williams a reason to call CP&P (or anyone) for help ever again but didn't know how to prove everything was okay.

Maybe if she did well in this class, not only would she be closer to understanding her dad, but Miss Williams would also see that she was fine. Maybe she could get her dad to come to the Fall Festival, and look at her painting and be okay, and everyone—including her classmates and Miss Williams—would see that.

Miss Williams was speaking with Jeremy about his project. He didn't look particularly into it. He sighed, running a hand through his cowlick as he turned to Fig and said, "Can your dad come interrupt so we can get out of art class again?"

"*Jeremy!*" Miss Williams snapped, startling Fig (and her classmates, who immediately went silent). Miss Williams never yelled, and the back of Fig's neck grew warm as she felt the attention drawn to her. "Go sit down, *now*, and get started on your work."

Jeremy looked confused, but he didn't need to be told twice.

Miss Williams looked up with her kind eyes and an apologetic smile, which made Fig gaze down at her toes. "I'm sorry about that, Fig. That sort of thing is not okay, and—"

Fig quickly held out the big, heavy art book for Miss Williams to take, stopping her from saying anything more. Jeremy was just being a pest. Miss Williams was the one who was turning nothing into *something*.

"Did you get a good look?" Miss Williams asked, taking the hint. Fig nodded. "Find anything helpful?"

"Do you have any more books on Vincent van Gogh? I Googled him, but our internet's slow."

Miss Williams smiled her wide, toothy smile. "Van Gogh, huh? That's an interesting choice. What about Van Gogh caught your eye? A lot of students your age are drawn to the swirls and colors in *The Starry Night*. Or his sunflowers."

"I liked the ones he painted of himself. And the one of the yellow house."

Fig wanted to paint the look on Miss Williams's face and keep it forever: her eyes sparkling with a real smile that was just for Fig. It was the kind of look that had no pity, and that she hadn't seen in nearly two weeks. "You surprise me, Fig. You know, he actually shared his wing of the yellow house with another artist, Paul Gauguin. It was a very formative time in Van Gogh's life, both personally and as an artist," Miss Williams said, and then laughed. "They drove each other crazy."

Fig wasn't surprised. She knew full well how difficult living with an artist could be.

"I don't think I have anything else here, but let's see if we can't find something for you to check out from the library." Miss Williams opened her laptop, clicked away at the keys, and before the class was over, wrote down five different book titles for Fig.

The problem, Fig realized as she stared at the sheet of paper in front of her, still blank, was that even though she was interested in Van Gogh, she still didn't understand a thing about art—and still didn't have a clue about what to paint. So at the end of the school day when she got off the bus (she knew her dad had lessons to give), she decided to go straight to the library.

The library wasn't large, but it was big enough, and she hoped she'd find most of the books Miss Williams wrote down. It wasn't that busy—just a few people at computers and some parents with their young children browsing shelves. Fig wished her father were the kind of dad to do a project like this with her, so she didn't have to do it alone. But she was used to this. She had a library card that had miles' worth of use from the time she spent last year reading about hurricanes and their typical patterns—and how often they happened in New Jersey.

Back then, a high school boy named Tom worked behind the library counter after school, always looking like he was on the verge of falling asleep. But now, as Fig walked up to the counter and stood on her tiptoes to see over the top, there was a teenage girl standing there. Fig waited for her to stop sorting books and notice she was there.

The girl, like Tom the year before, wore the local private high school uniform: a green plaid shirt, which she wore unbuttoned, with a purple tank top underneath. Her dirty-blond hair was pulled back in a loose ponytail, wisps falling over her face the way Fig's did on the days her dad's braids were too loose to stay in place.

"Excuse me?" Fig worked up the nerve to say.

The girl leaned against the counter, looking at Fig. Her eyes were dark, and Fig felt herself blushing under their gaze. "What can I do for you?" she said. Her name tag read: Hannah.

"What happened to Tom?"

"My brother left for college, and I was lucky enough to get his job for the next two years until *I* can leave." Hannah didn't sound like she really thought it was "lucky." "What do you need?"

Fig placed the paper with the Van Gogh book titles from Miss Williams on the counter. "Can you help me find these books, please?"

Hannah sighed, but she took the list anyway. She scanned the titles and tilted her head to one side. "You from the art club?"

"Um, no. I have a school project."

"On Vincent van Gogh?"

Fig nodded.

Hannah grew quiet, and Fig was about to give up. But Hannah shrugged and said, “Cool.” Fig felt warm inside from the approval.

Hannah clicked away at the computer. “Okay, follow me.” She didn’t wait to make sure Fig was behind her as she headed toward the stacks of nonfiction books on the other side of the library. Fig did her best to keep up.

Hannah kept her eyes on the shelves as she looked for the books, and Fig kept hers on Hannah. Hannah had three piercings in one ear, and none of the earrings matched. Fig liked that. She liked how Hannah kept trying to push the loose strands of hair behind her ear, even though they didn’t stay there.

Hannah handed Fig a book, and Fig got caught staring. “What?” Hannah asked.

Fig’s eyes were wide as she blurted, “Your earrings don’t match.”

Hannah laughed. Fig’s cheeks were on fire.

They found three out of the five books Miss Williams wrote down. When all three books were in her hands, Fig said “thank you” so many times she was pretty sure Hannah was laughing *at* her. She thought she might go up in flames.

"You know, you've got an overdue book," Hannah said as she swiped Fig's library card. "Like, *way* overdue. Like I probably shouldn't let you take these books until you either pay for or return it."

Fig knew *exactly* what book it was. It was about storms from New Jersey's history, about the biggest ones to hit the coast, and about the damage each one had done. The book had caught Fig's dad's eyes (she figured he was pulled in by the photographs). And the water damage the book sustained while in her dad's arms as he stood too close to the ocean made it too damaged to return—the words bleeding together and the spine weathered and disintegrating. It was now hidden away under Fig's bed.

"Can I take these books and bring the money for the other one when I return them?" Fig asked. Her dad said he would pay for the overdue book, but he kept forgetting. "Please?"

Hannah sighed. "All right. Just if Mrs. Gregory asks, you better not tell her I said it was okay." She paused, and Fig thought she was going to change her mind. But instead, she winked at Fig. "It'll be our secret."

Fig was practically sweating. Hannah had a great wink. "Thank you!" Fig said.

"Don't forget!" Hannah said.

"I won't!"

Fig started to walk away, but she couldn't take her eyes off Hannah. Which was why she immediately bumped into the boy behind her, successfully dropping all three books in the process. "Oh, sorry," she said as she bent to pick them up again.

The boy, she realized, was Danny from school. He bent down to help her. "I was trying to get your attention, but I guess you didn't see me," he said.

"No. Sorry." They both stood, and he looked at the book now in his hands. Fig turned back to Hannah, hoping that Hannah hadn't noticed how clumsy she was. But Hannah was focused on shelving books again, Fig already forgotten.

Danny swooped his bangs to the side with a quick jerk of his head. "You're reading about Van Gogh? Are you coming to art club?"

"It's for class, for Miss Williams," Fig told him.

"Oh," he said, and then glanced around the room. "Where's your dad?"

Fig scowled. Danny, like all of Fig's friends and classmates, probably had a head full of questions. "He's not here," she said.

"Oh," Danny said again.

She didn't like the disappointed look on his face. "I have to go," she said.

"Wait! You should come to art club," he said quickly, before she could leave. "We meet here, at the library. That's why I'm here. We don't talk about Van Gogh, but we learn how to draw."

Fig didn't say that she thought Danny already knew how to draw, that he was already probably the best student in art class—even if he constantly changed his mind about what to draw or paint, and his desk was always covered in eraser bits. "Do you know anything about Van Gogh?" she asked.

"I just know some of his paintings," Danny said. "Oh—and that he cut off his ear."

"He did *what*?"

"Yeah, I think he was crazy or something."

Danny continued talking, continued sweeping aside his shaggy hair, but Fig did not continue listening. She held the books in her hands a little tighter; she didn't want to open them and learn that Van Gogh was crazy. She didn't *want* him to be crazy.

He already reminded her too much of her dad.

"I have to go," she said, cutting Danny off. "I'll see you at school."

Fig left the library, holding the books tightly and close to her chest with one hand and tugging at her earlobe with the other.

Fig's immediate plan was to get home, check that her dad had both his ears, and read the Van Gogh books to learn that he was a normal, well-respected man. Besides, Fig told herself, just because a painter from more than a hundred years ago happened to *look* like her dad, it didn't mean they were alike in any other ways.

Fig was so caught up in her thoughts, she didn't register anything around her. Not the cars that drove by or the crunch of leaves under her feet. Nothing registered, until she was close enough to her home to hear the slightly out-of-tune keys of her dad's piano ringing out across the front lawn and down the walkway and into her ears. It was a pretty tune, one that she had heard over and over in different keys, different patterns, and she couldn't help but smile at the sound of it. She noticed that, across the street, Mark was doing the same.

He was standing by his truck in the driveway, his hand gripping the toolbox in the bed of it, as if he had been about to take the truck out but got distracted and forgot. He was staring across the street, at Fig's house—listening to Fig's dad's music—and Fig's shoulders tensed.

"What are you doing?" Fig called.

Mark startled and turned to look at her. "That your dad?" he asked.

"Yeah, with one of his students. He's a musician."

Mark nodded. "He's good."

"He's great," Fig fired back. "Sometimes you can't tell that now, but he is."

"I can tell," Mark said, and Fig didn't know what to make of that.

They listened to her dad play the same line again and again—and then his student repeated it slower as the sun started to fall behind the trees, leaving them both covered in shadows.

Still, Mark kept listening.

Fig thought about asking him if he knew anything about brilliant musicians, about royalties, about income. If he knew anything about Van Gogh, or anything about being crazy, or being sad—or just plain *worried* that all those things might come together and swallow them all up someday.

But eventually, Mark would hear from their other neighbors, and he would see her dad walking and talking to himself on his way to stand at the ocean. He would realize that sometimes her dad went weeks without leaving the house, sometimes went longer without changing his clothes or shaving his face. He would hear the stretches of days that her dad went without students, when the piano fell out of tune—and still he played, the music not quite right and slightly alarming. He would realize what everyone on her block already knew, and he would write off her dad like everyone else did.

Fig did not want Mark to ever learn all these things and then look at her, to make the connection that Miss Williams had.

Her dad's music came to a stop, and the art books started to feel heavy in her arms. Fig checked her cell phone for the time and figured his lesson must be ending. She turned back to Mark and gave him a shoulder shrug and half smile. "I'll see you around," she said, and quickly turned to head up the walkway to the front door.

A car turned onto the street and into Fig's driveway. And before Fig could reach the knob, the door swung open, revealing a girl who looked about her age with thick curly hair and bright blue glasses. She was carrying sheet music in her hands. "Oh!" the girl said. She had freckles on her nose. "Hello."

"Hi," Fig replied. Her dad's students usually didn't speak much to her, and they were more often than not a lot older.

The girl waved at the car in the driveway, and Fig turned to watch the woman inside it—the girl's mother, probably—wave back. "I'm Molly. Mr. Arnold's your dad, right? I saw your picture on the walls inside."

"Yeah," Fig said carefully. "He's my dad."

"This was my first lesson," Molly continued. "I'm trying to get a head start so I can get into MCPA in a couple years. You know, the performing arts high school?" Fig was about to respond, but Molly's mom honked a quick little honk, and Molly nodded in her direction. "I gotta go, but seriously—your dad's incredible. You're so lucky." She ran down the front steps and the walkway toward her mom's car, and Fig watched her go, holding the art books in her arms a little tighter.

Molly's words made Fig smile, but she couldn't understand why they also made her want to cry.

When Fig got home from school the next day, there was a different car in the driveway. She didn't think her dad had a lesson, and they never had visitors. She dropped her backpack on the front lawn and ran to the door.

She quickly swung it open, keeping her shoes on as she hurried into the house, where she found her dad and a man she didn't know standing in the living room. The man wore a nice, crisp shirt and a tie, and he held a folder and plastic container in his hands. Her dad wore one of his wrinkled white undershirts and jeans, his feet bare and his hands buried deep in his pockets. They both turned and looked at her.

"Why don't you go get your homework started, love?" her dad said, his eyes pleading.

"What's going on?" Fig asked, not moving. The TV was on, and a radar map of Tropical Storm Diane took up the full screen.

"Hello," the man said. "No need to worry. I'm John, with Child Protection and Permanency. They explained to you about these visits?"

Fig's dad stood straighter as he looked from Fig to John and back again. "She knows," he said. "I'll take care of it."

"Dad," Fig said, unable to take her eyes away from John and the package in his hand. She wasn't ready for this. She hadn't been at home all day. She didn't get to check in on her dad to make sure he was all there, and the TV was on and they were talking about the approaching storm and what if her dad said something about that? Did this man, John, already know about what happened last year? The last CP&P lady who came to the door said they had a file from last time—had John read that file? Did he have it with him? Would he think it could happen again? *Could* it happen again?

She looked over at the calendar on the wall, at all the crossed-out dates, at the September header that meant there was still so much time left in which things could go wrong.

"It's all right, Fig," her dad said, getting her attention. "Go inside and start your homework, and I'll come get you when we're done here, okay?"

He was rarely cross with her, but there was a bitter edge in his voice that stopped her short. He gave her a smile, but it didn't look right, and his face was flushed, and a drop of sweat was dripping down one side of his forehead. Fig didn't want to leave him. She wanted to stay right there and make sure that he didn't say anything damaging, make sure John didn't hurt him, make sure nothing went wrong.

"Dad," she said again.

"Go, Fig."

He left no room for argument, so she did as she was told.

That didn't stop her from keeping a close watch anyway. She kept her door open just enough so she could sit on her bed and tilt her head to see down the hall, where John opened up a small plastic container and handed her dad what looked like a small toothbrush. "Place this between your lower cheek and gum," John said. Fig watched as her dad did as he was told. "And keep that there for a moment while it collects your saliva."

Fig remembered the first CP&P lady telling them that someone would show up to administer drug tests. She knew her dad didn't do drugs—he didn't even drink—but she didn't like watching him do this. She wondered if that was what Miss Williams thought the day he turned up looking for her in art class. If Miss Williams called CP&P because she thought her dad wasn't sober.

John told her dad he could take the toothbrush drug test out of his mouth and then took it from him. They stood there in silence for a moment—her dad's hands fidgeting against his thighs as John's eyes remained on the test in his hand. Fig knew her dad didn't do drugs, but she found herself holding her breath anyway.

"Okay, Mr. Arnold, you're all set," John finally said. Fig breathed easier, and her dad exhaled loudly enough for her to hear it. John reached into the folder he had tucked under his armpit (*Is that the file?*) and pulled out some papers. "Here are some brochures and referrals for doctors that come highly recommended. A lot of them have wait lists, so it could take a while to get an appointment, and you'll have to sort through to see which accept your insurance. You want to get this taken care of quickly so that we can see that there's progress when we pop in."

Her dad took the papers, staring down at them in his hands. "Right."

"If you need any assistance, here's a number you can call. We can help guide you through this, Mr. Arnold. It's important."

"Right," her dad said again.

Fig moved away from the door to sit on her bed, listening as her dad walked John to the door, listening as the door opened and closed. She even listened for John's car as it drove away.

Her dad came and knocked softly on her door. "Fig? You okay?" he asked as he entered. He had her backpack in his hands. "I found this outside."

"Thanks." Fig offered him her best attempt at a smile. She couldn't hold it very long. "Is this going to happen a lot? Are they going to come by a lot?"

He sighed. "I don't know. I hope not."

She fiddled with the zipper on her backpack. The random visits were what scared her the most. She didn't know how her dad would be feeling at any given moment. She didn't know exactly when any future hurricane would make landfall. "Me too."

Her dad hovered at the threshold, playing with the doorknob that was loose and wiggled when he touched it. "I don't want you to worry about any of this, all right?

It'll get sorted. I . . ." He drifted off with a shrug. "Please try not to worry."

Fig glanced at her now-open backpack on the floor, the library book of Van Gogh's letters poking out behind her folder.

"Okay?" he asked, still toying with her doorknob.

Fig looked up at him and nodded. "Okay."

# LANDSCAPE UNDER A STORMY SKY

"What am I in the eyes of most people?" Vincent van Gogh wrote to his brother. "A nonentity, an eccentric or an unpleasant person—somebody who has no position in society and never will have, in short, the lowest of the low."

Fig's eyes were blurry as she struggled to read the words, written by Van Gogh but echoing in her mind in her dad's voice: "Though I am often in the depths of misery, there is still calmness, pure harmony and music inside me."

The reading wasn't easy—Van Gogh's letters were lengthy and confusing and difficult for Fig—but these words she understood. They expressed something she was familiar with. Van Gogh was an outcast to most people, just like her dad. And, just like her dad, he was comforted by art and the music inside of him.

Fig closed the book that sat on her lap as she rode the school bus, blinking back tears. She leaned her forehead against the window to stare outside at the trees and traffic lights that knocked about in the harsh winds.

The storm was finally coming.

As Fig's bus drove across the highway that separated her town from the town where her school stood, she looked at the parking lots of the shopping centers that they rode by. Those lots were full, and people walked from the stores to their cars, carrying water bottles and canned goods and everything else needed in case Tropical Storm Diane moved, as predicted, up along their shores. Lines at the gas stations would grow longer and longer. Fig and her dad planned to board up their windows when she got home.

Fig's fingers toyed with her earlobe as she reopened the book of Van Gogh's letters. "My mind," Van Gogh wrote, "is driven towards these things with an irresistible momentum."

Just like her dad was always pulled toward a storm.

However, except for the growing winds, the clichéd "calm before the storm" was holding true. Fig walked down the hallway of her school, past the windows where sunlight continued to break through the darkening clouds. She tried to focus on that, on the bits of blue sky she could see from inside the school building, and not the anxiety that rolled in her stomach like the storm she knew would also roll in soon.

"Did you decide on what to paint yet?" Danny said, taking Fig by surprise as he jogged from the other end of the hallway to fall in step beside her.

"What?"

"For Miss Williams," he said. "Are you going to paint something like Van Gogh?"

"Oh. I don't know what I'm painting yet," Fig said. She was reading a lot but still at a loss what to do with the research. "I just wanted to learn more about him, for now."

"Did you? Learn about him, I mean."

She sighed. "Well, you were right. He *did* cut off his ear."

"I thought so."

"He was sick, though, I think," Fig said, and slowed to a stop. They reached the school auditorium, where Fig had gym class. "That's not the same as being crazy."

"What was wrong with him?"

"I don't . . . The books are hard to read, and I'm still trying to figure it out. But he was just sick." Fig frowned.

She didn't know the words to explain. "He couldn't help it."

Danny bit the inside of his cheek. "What about your dad?" he asked.

It shouldn't have shocked her that her classmates were figuring out her dad was sick, but still, Danny's question took Fig's breath away. "He's *fine*," she said, and pushed open the auditorium door with more force than necessary. It swung open hard and clanked against the wall.

Danny hurried after her as she headed inside. "I didn't mean . . . Wait, Fig, slow down."

The late bell rang, but Fig stopped anyway. She turned to look expectantly at Danny.

"Are you going to Ava Washington's Halloween party?" he said. "It's obviously not until next month, but everyone's already talking about going."

Fig blinked. She wasn't expecting that. Nor had she known everyone was talking about the party. Across the auditorium, Ava and the other girls were already sitting on the gym floor, dressed in their gym clothes and carelessly rolling a basketball back and forth. No one had talked with Fig about the party, at least.

A few of the other girls in their class pushed past Fig to go get changed. She was blocking the door to the locker room. “I don’t know,” Fig said carefully. “I’m not sure I’m invited.”

“Well, I’m inviting you,” Danny said. “My mom and I can pick you up if you want. We can go together.”

Fig hesitated. The wind from outside suddenly blew hard against the windows, and the sound echoed throughout the auditorium. Fig jumped; worry vibrated through her arms and legs like pins and needles as she looked up, sunlight now hidden by dark clouds, shadows covering the gymnasium.

“Are you afraid of storms?” Danny asked.

Fig took a deep breath, and confided in someone for the very first time. “It’s my dad. Storms make him . . .” She winced, not knowing what to say that would keep Danny from laughing at her. That would keep him from thinking about that day in art class.

But Danny didn’t laugh. “I hope he’s okay.”

Fig felt like she might cry. “Thanks.”

Danny smiled wide, the gap between his teeth front and center.

The dark gray clouds eventually completely covered the sky, leaving the town shrouded in gloom. The winds hit against the windows of her school bus, whistling loudly.

The rain started, the sound of it against the metal of the bus bringing back the pins and needles in Fig's arms and legs, making her wonder what her dad loved about those sounds. The rain wasn't heavy, not yet, but it was steady enough that as she watched it fall, Fig's stomach started to hurt. She wanted to be home, with her dad, boarding up their windows together, making sure everything was safe.

The rain and wind picked up even more as she exited the bus, and she held the hood of her jacket in place as she ran toward her house. No extra cars, no CP&P visit. She saw Mark across the street—boarding up his own windows and preparing his home for what may come—and she returned the wave he gave her. "You guys need help boarding up?" he called.

"We've got it!" Fig yelled.

"Stay safe," he returned as Fig ran into her house for shelter.

The wind blew the door closed behind her with a loud slam. "Dad? I'm home! Did you get the boards ready for the windows?"

No response. Fig tossed her backpack to the side, kicking off her shoes and unzipping her jacket as she began to search the rooms for her dad. "Dad?" she called again, checking the couch and his bed and the other places where he sought solace. Her dad being asleep wouldn't be ideal—she was too small to get the house ready by herself—but she would deal with that once she found him.

But she couldn't find him.

And then she noticed that his shoes were gone.

Her stomach sank and hurt, and she knew—she *knew*—that he loved a storm, he loved to watch a storm, he loved to stand at the beach with his toes in the waves, staring out at the sea as the storm rolled in, and she couldn't call the police like she did last time, not with CP&P breathing down their necks, not with the file of what happened during last year's hurricane and this year's art class. He was out there alone, and she would have to find him and drag him home, or he would be stuck out there, and Fig *hated* storms, and and and . . .

She quickly grabbed her shoes and pulled them on, nearly forgetting her jacket but grabbing it at the last second as she ran back out the door, which slammed again behind her. The rain was coming down harder now, and the wind whipped her hair in front of her face.

"Hey!" Mark called from across the street. "What are you doing? Get back inside!"

He was at his front door but moved quickly across his yard, then stopping short, as if he were about to run across the street to scoop her up before realizing that he had no right to. Fig wasn't about to let him stop her. "I have to go find my dad!"

"What?" he called, moving closer.

"My dad!" she shouted through the wind. "He's not home . . . He sometimes . . . I don't have time for this!"

"You have to get inside," he said, coming closer, and Fig balled her hands into fists, wanting to cry. Ms. Minkle would have ignored her.

"He won't come back if I don't get him!" She was grateful for the raindrops for a moment because they fell down her cheeks, so it didn't matter that her tears fell with them. Two houses down, a branch on one of the Ramirezes' trees—one that was already splintered from the last big storm—cracked and fell and blew against their house with a rattle that caused her to jump, caused her stomach to hurt even more, caused her to tug hard on her earlobe.

Mark was suddenly standing in front of her, his hands clamping tight on her shoulders as he bent over to her level, the rain falling off his short hair as he blinked the drops out of his eyes. "Get inside. *Now*. I'll go get him."

"He always goes down—"

"Down by the water, right?" he interrupted. "I've seen him during my runs."

She nodded, and the rain fell harder, and Mark practically pushed her to get her to go back into the house. "I've got him," he said as he took off running.

Fig didn't know what to do. It was her job to look after her dad; she couldn't just sit idly by. She thought she might be sick, and her ear was sore from her tugging on it, and she could barely see out the window, could no longer see Mark, would not be able to tell if he found her dad, if her dad was okay, or if the sea finally swallowed him up and for extra measure took Mark right along with him.

A gust of wind blew hard against the window, startling her away from it. She and her dad hadn't boarded them up. They didn't have time now to prepare. The storm was coming, was *here*, and would only get worse. She glanced at the calendar. September wasn't even over yet. How on earth would they make it to the end of hurricane season?

Fig unzipped the front pocket of her backpack and pulled out her cell phone. It would be so easy to call the police. *Should* she call the police? They saved him last time, but the neighbors all saw, and CP&P stopped by the next morning and started a file that only made things worse when Miss Williams called them. Because they already knew Tim Arnold, already knew that he was fractured and Fig might not be safe. But she was safe, wasn't she? He loved her and she loved him and sometimes he just . . . *he just couldn't help it*.

Why did he do this? What did he see and hear out there that she couldn't? What went on in his mind that made him do this to her?

Her fingers hovered over the phone keys as the wind blew harder and lightning lit up the sky. She sat on the floor, her knees pulled into her chest. She closed her eyes and silently counted to see how far away it struck—*One Mississippi, two Mississippi, three Mississippi*—until thunder echoed throughout the room. Her dad knew she hated storms, he knew what he did to them last time, and she was cold, and angry, and *how could he do this to her*?

No wonder her mother left. Maybe CP&P should go find her. Fig hated herself for thinking it. Hated her dad more, in that moment, for making her think it.

But then the door burst open, wind and rain blowing in with Mark as he practically carried her dad over the threshold. Her dad, who was home and found but still looked *lost*. His eyes were foggy and searching and confused as the drops of water from his soaked hair and overly scruffy beard dripped onto the carpet. Mark was holding all her dad's weight, his arms wrapped tightly around him. Her dad wasn't making any attempt to help

Mark support him. Her dad just leaned in to him, letting Mark carry him.

Mark, while still holding her dad, stripped off his soaked jacket and tossed it to the floor and then removed her dad's. Her dad was shivering, trembling, and Mark stripped off his Michigan State sweatshirt and pulled it down over her dad's head, and her dad just let him, just let this stranger move him like a rag doll, as if he weren't quite all there to do anything about it anyway.

Fig wanted to cry and wrap her arms around him and never let go.

"His bedroom?" Mark prompted, snapping Fig out of her thoughts. She nodded fiercely and led him down the hall, opening the door to her dad's bedroom. Mark half carried, half dragged her dad in, and Fig grabbed a towel to dry him off as Mark pulled at his wet shoes and socks and pants, leaving her dad in Mark's mostly dry sweatshirt and his boxers.

Together, they gently helped her dad onto the bed, pushing lightly so he would lie back as Mark lifted his feet. Then Fig pushed Mark away to step in. This was her dad, her job, and she knew how to do it. She tried not to think about what Mark saw when he looked around her dad's bedroom, if he saw the endless scattered pages of songs half composed and erased and started all over, if he noticed the empty mugs on the nightstand, the dirty laundry on the floor.

Her dad was watching her through half-lidded, unfocused eyes as she reached over to pull at his duvet to cover him with it. She tucked him in and leaned over him to place a kiss on his still too-rough and stubbly face. Even Fig had exceptions to her own rules.

He blinked at her as she moved away. Mumbled a quiet, "Love you, darling."

She blinked back her tears. "Double it." It was a soft challenge in the quiet room.

He closed his eyes, and for a moment she thought he'd just fallen asleep. She stepped away from his bed and moved toward the door, reaching for Mark's hand to pull him out with her. Mark had seen enough tonight.

Fig's hand was on the doorknob when she heard it. "Love you, love you."

Mark followed her to the living room, sat down on the opposite side of the couch from Fig. She knew he was waiting for an explanation, and knew even more that she owed him one. He had weathered the storm for her dad—for *her*—and he was wet, and probably cold in only his T-shirt and jeans, and oh, she should have thought to offer him a dry sweatshirt. She had wanted to protect her dad from one more neighbor, from one more person who might be cruel or a threat. Instead, she had pulled that neighbor into the middle of something she herself sometimes wanted out of, his hair dripping water down his face and onto his shirt because of a man—her dad—who got lost out in the storm.

The wind thrashing against the window was loud, and her voice was quiet and not exactly steady as she said, "I can get you one of my dad's sweatshirts if you want."

"Finola . . ."

She couldn't look at him. She didn't know how to start this conversation; more importantly, she didn't know how to get out of it.

The power suddenly blinked out, and even though it was only a moment before it powered back on, she found herself skidding closer to Mark, not quite close enough to touch but close enough to intrude on his personal space. He didn't move away. It gave her the courage to look up into his eyes, and she immediately wished she hadn't. They were soft, and sad, and reminded her of her dad's.

"Fig," he tried again, "what's wrong with your dad?"

The question was so blunt and honest, it knocked the wind right out of her. *"Nothing."* Her voice was cruel, even to her own ears, but Mark had too many pieces of a puzzle that could take her dad away.

"Fig." He kept saying her name, the nickname she hadn't yet given him permission to use.

"He doesn't mean it," she whispered, and then repeated the words she used with Danny earlier: "He just . . . can't help it."

The rain came down harder, the thunder rolling in behind it. The drops continued to pelt the window, which rattled in the wind. Fig wanted to be older, or bigger, or *brave enough* to have boarded the windows up by herself. The power went out again, and this time it stayed out. She started shivering. She wished her dad were the type of dad who could protect her during a storm. She wished her mom were the type of mom who never would have left her.

"Will you stay?" she asked Mark without thinking. "Please? Stay until the storm passes?"

Mark hesitated, and Fig knew she had overstepped, knew she should take it back, knew she should probably be defending her dad, making excuses for him, keeping Mark at a distance so that he wouldn't turn around and call Fig's school or the police or social services. They were already out of second chances. They already had one too many red flags for CP&P to ignore.

But then he slowly exhaled. "Yeah."

The tension left Fig's shoulders as she released the deep breath she was holding. She curled her legs underneath her, and cuddled against the couch. Mark grabbed the old tatty throw blanket draped over the back to cover her.

Together, they waited out the storm.

# 6

# WHEAT FIELDS AFTER THE RAIN

FIG WAS AWOKEN FROM A RESTLESS SLEEP BY HER dad's panicked voice, his accent pronounced as it always was in moments when he was thrown for a loop. "What are you doing in my house? With my *daughter*?"

Her dad was bleary from sleep, his hair matted on one side and sticking out on the other from falling asleep with it wet. He was still wearing Mark's much too large sweatshirt, and he slouched to one side, looking at them through his narrowed eyes (though from anger or tiredness, Fig wasn't sure). Honestly, even if Mark were a neighborhood predator, her dad wasn't exactly all that threatening.

At some point during the storm, Fig had started to use Mark as a pillow, and she could now feel him stiffen and attempt to pull away, which she figured would be the appropriate gesture if this were a typical situation. "He brought you home, Dad. You're literally wearing the clothes off his back."

Her dad's eyebrows pinched together, and he looked at her as if she were daft. But then she could almost see the fog clearing from his gaze, and Fig exhaled deeply in relief. Her dad looked down, his fingers plucking at the white letters of Mark's green sweatshirt.

The anger and confusion seemed to vanish, and her dad was left looking much smaller. Fig had seen him do a lot of things that most children didn't witness their parents doing, but she hadn't seen him blush very often. He stood there now with his ears turning pink. "Oh," he mumbled. "It's comfy." His fingers continued playing with the letters against his chest, as if they were piano keys, and his eyes moved to the window. "How was the storm?"

Fig burst into tears.

Her dad was suddenly next to her on the couch, pulling her nearly onto his lap, holding her head against the letters of Mark's sweatshirt. "I'm sorry, love. I'm sorry. I don't know what else to say," he murmured against her hair as he rocked her. "I love you, I love you. I'm so sorry."

Fig wiped at her tears, reveling in the fact that her dad was here, and whole, and holding her, and she inhaled his scent, which mingled with a wood smell that came from Mark's sweatshirt. With her face pressed against her dad's chest, she turned slightly to look at Mark, who was still sitting with them on the couch, watching them with his soft eyes, clasping his hands together in his lap as he sat ramrod straight.

She pulled away slightly to properly look at Mark, who caught her dad's attention, too, as they all fully realized the awkwardness of the situation. Things that had gone unexplained now needed explaining, things that could get Fig and her dad in trouble. Fig should not have asked Mark to stay, because any adult who would walk away from this, without looking back, after everything he witnessed last night, would not be a responsible one.

So she had learned from Miss Williams.

"Why don't you go get ready for school?" her dad said. He wasn't naïve, and Fig knew a dismissal when she heard one.

"It's Saturday."

"Then go shower and change, and I'll make us breakfast."

There was a conversation to be had, and Fig was worried about how well her dad was going to have it. She glanced warily at Mark, and her dad gave her a gentle push. Neither of them said a word as she padded away to her bedroom.

The first thing Fig noticed when she left her bedroom, her hair still wet from the shower and wearing a semi-wrinkled flannel shirt that at least passed her sniff test, was that Mark was still there, and the police (or a CP&P person or an ambulance or someone with a straitjacket) weren't.

The second thing she noticed was that the house had the faint aroma of bacon, and the voices from the kitchen weren't shouting at each other, weren't desperate or angry or sad but just sort of . . . conversational. As if they were actually two adults rationally discussing a situation in which she often felt out of control, despite her familiarity with it. One that Mark was new to, one that currently put the ball (the entire court, really) in his hands. She tiptoed quietly across the hallway toward the kitchen and paused outside the wall that separated it from the living room to cross yet another day off the calendar. September 21. She was ready for the month to end.

"It's those big eyes that take up half her face. Hard to turn away from," she heard her dad say. "I get that."

Fig leaned in, her ear against the doorway. She wasn't above eavesdropping.

"It's not just . . . I mean, yes, it was her, running headfirst into a storm. But it was you, too." That was Mark. "I had a feeling something wasn't okay. Maybe I should have said something sooner, but . . . it's not my place, is it? I wanted to help, is all."

"Nearly gave me a heart attack to see you curled up with Fig, though."

"She asked me to stay. Couldn't say no."

"But you could have left before now," her dad responded.

Fig pressed herself closer to the wall, wanting to hear what Mark had to say, why Mark was still here. "I didn't know if you . . ." Mark paused. "I wasn't sure if I could leave her with . . ."

*He didn't know if he could leave her alone with her dad.* Which was what everyone was wondering these days, wasn't it?

She wanted her dad to respond to that. She wanted him to defend himself, or to tell Mark that he was fine, and they didn't need more people butting in, even if Fig had invited him in the first place.

Instead, he cleared his throat to say, louder than necessary, "Fig, darling, when you're done spying on your dear dad, come have some breakfast."

She pushed herself off the wall and plodded into the kitchen, where her dad was standing—still wearing Mark's sweatshirt—by the stove, poking at the pan full of bacon strips with a spatula. Mark was sitting at their small (but good enough for them) kitchen table. The table had just two chairs. Their kitchen really only had room for two people to comfortably sit and eat, and that had always suited them just fine.

Fig took the chair Mark wasn't in, with a plate of scrambled eggs her dad prepared on the table in front of her. Across from her, Mark was nursing a cup of tea. He didn't particularly strike Fig as the tea type, so she could only assume he was being polite about drinking it. He was making her nervous; she didn't know what he thought of their situation, and she didn't want to find out. She wanted him to go home, and she wanted her dad to promise there would never be another storm, just clear bright skies and sun from now on.

"Bacon?" her dad asked.

She cut him a glare, didn't even feel bad about it when his shoulders sagged and he put the frying pan down. He went to stuff his hands in the pocket of Mark's sweatshirt but then looked as if he just remembered he was *still wearing* said sweatshirt, and he lowered his hands to his sides instead. "Right. You're angry with me."

"You scared me, Dad."

"I know, love. I know." The one thing she always appreciated was that he didn't deny; he never tried to justify. He *did* know. They both did. They just didn't know what to do about it.

"You can't keep doing this, Dad. I almost called the police! What if they saw you like that again? What if CP and P showed up? There's still ten weeks until hurricane season is over, Dad, that's ten weeks before they come back and decide, and what if—"

Her dad looked over at Mark, and Fig swallowed the rest of her words.

Still, he didn't make excuses. "What can I do to make it up to you?"

Fig knew she could have asked him to get her an original Van Gogh painting, and he would have done everything in his power to make it happen. But as she looked at him, wrapped in another man's sweatshirt, still more than half a mess from the wind and rain that had assaulted his hair, she knew exactly what she wanted. "You can shave."

Mark barked a laugh, which startled Fig.

Her dad looked over at Mark and fought back a smile, bringing a hand up to run through his more-beard-than-stubble. Then he dropped his hand and looked down, letting his fingers dance for a moment before clasping them together. Even Fig could see that he was still a little shaky. "Probably not a good idea today. Rain check? Tomorrow?"

But Fig stood her ground. "No. Today. Right now."

He put on a smile for show, his eyes moving to Mark's before finding hers again. "I can't, Fig."

"Then I'll do it." She squared her jaw, daring either of them to disagree with her. Her dad opened his mouth, she was sure, to try to. She didn't let him. "If you really want to make it up to me, this is how you can do it."

She almost felt guilty about how easily he conceded.

"Give Mark some bacon," she said. "I'll go get what we need."

Mark was still sitting there at the table when she returned, and Fig avoided eye contact with him. She wanted him to go home—didn't he see they were fine now? But he stayed and watched, chewing on his bacon and eggs (and still nursing that cup of tea) as she sat her dad in the other chair and lathered him up. She got shaving cream on her shirt (and his pants), and he wasn't exactly the type to sit still. But he didn't object as she picked up his razor, even though she had never actually done this before.

How hard could it be? She wet the razor, turning on the faucet at the sink, and then reached for her dad's chin to steady his face, her fingers slipping a bit before getting a good grip. She held her breath, and felt herself almost cringing as she went to make the first swipe, and—

"Wait, wait. Stop," Mark said, and despite herself, Fig sighed in deep relief at the interruption. "I can't watch this—give me the razor."

"Oh, thank God," her dad said, and Fig scowled at him. "I'm sorry. You know I'd do anything for you, but I rather like my face."

The part of her that forgave her dad anything already forgave him for the storm, especially since he was willing to let her possibly cut up his face just for the sake of her forgiveness. Still, she huffed as she handed the razor over to Mark, the near stranger from the yellow house across the street, who now knew more than enough about them to gossip with the neighbors.

"Man's saved my life twice in less than twenty-four hours, now. Should have made him something better than scrambled eggs," her dad joked. Fig wasn't all that amused.

Neither was Mark, it seemed. He leaned in to reach for her dad's face, taking a dish towel from where it hung over the sink and wiping at some of the mess Fig had made with the shaving cream. There was something gentle but deliberate about the way he then held the razor, and the way he looked at her dad's cheeks and chin as if he were studying them, as if he were going to carve his face from scratch into something fresh and new.

Fig found she was envious. Where she made a mess, Mark approached the task like an artist.

Mark started, and they were all kind of stiff and uneasy and quiet, listening to the sound of the razor run through cream against skin, until her dad let out a sudden soft giggle, which Mark followed with a shake of his head and a laugh of his own. The situation was kind of awkward, maybe even odd. Fig's closed-off dad and stranger-danger neighbor were sitting in the kitchen, so close together their noses were practically touching—and Fig unexpectedly found herself laughing, too.

And then they were all laughing a little stronger, and Mark was holding her dad's face tight, saying, "Stay still before I nick an artery."

Her dad tried hard to sit still and managed to hold it together long enough for Mark to finish the job. He chucked the razor in the sink and grabbed the dish towel, holding it out for Fig. “Want to do the honors?”

Fig nodded, taking the towel and wiping the excess shaving cream and leftover whiskers from her dad’s face. Once he was clean, she placed the towel on the counter and touched his cheeks, wanting to feel his smooth skin, studying the shape of his face now that he was no longer unkempt. He looked much healthier as her eyes met his.

“Better?” he asked, and she knew that he meant it, that simple question, and everything that it implied.

She threw her arms around his neck. “Love you, Dad.”

“Double it, darling.”

“Love you, love you.”

# LA BERCEUSE (WOMAN ROCKING A CRADLE)

FIG DIDN'T KNOW MUCH ABOUT HER MOTHER. WHAT she did know was that her parents met when her dad moved to New York City from "across the pond." That's what he always called the journey from England, when he was chasing more success and more money. He got both, plus a woman and a baby, and then lost everything but that baby.

Fig and her dad lived off echoes from that time—just barely recognizable, like the accent remaining in his voice—because his mind, she knew, suffered along the way.

She tried, as she struggled to read through that same book about Vincent van Gogh, to figure out a timeline of her dad's odd behaviors—tried to see if she could pinpoint a time in his life when things started to get blurry, like historians attempted to do with Van Gogh. There were big moments, sure, for each of them, but both the painter and her dad seemed to have traces of those intense moods always: found in Vincent's depressed letters to his brother and the sad look always present in her dad's eyes.

Fig read and learned what she could about the ways Van Gogh embarrassed his family, about the way his brother loved him, about how he lost faith in religion and found faith in art. She tried to understand his failures in relationships, his desire to sell his work, his erratic behavior. She was able to understand too easily the way his neighbors and the people who knew him called him mental, called him mad.

She read and read and read, the same letters over and over, skipping things that were too confusing and trying hard to learn the rest, trying to understand.

"The biggest difference," she confessed to Danny as they sat together at the library one afternoon, "is that Van Gogh finished a whole bunch of paintings, even when he was sickest. My dad hasn't finished anything in years."

"Have you figured out if it's Van-*go* or Van-*goff* yet?" Danny asked.

"What? No. I don't know. I keep saying *go*, but my dad always says *goff*."

"Okay. It doesn't matter. Anyway, maybe that's your dad's real problem? Art was really important to Van Gogh. Like music to your dad. It was basically what Van Gogh lived for."

"How do you know that?"

"It was in his letters, the ones he wrote to his brother." Danny pushed the book he was reading aside and pulled out his cell phone. "This is too hard to read. I'm just gonna Google."

Fig tried her best not to roll her eyes. "No, I know he said it in the letters. I mean how do *you* know about them?"

"I read about it online." Danny turned a little pink. "I wanted to try and help."

Fig smiled. She really liked having someone to confide in.

"I'm glad we can just text," Danny said. "Or Snapchat. Writing letters and then having to wait for them in the mail to check in with someone seems like a lot of work. It's bad enough when you have to wait for someone just to text you back."

Fig wondered what she would even say in a letter to her dad. *Dear Dad*, she'd start. *Please tell me what goes on in your head, about the music. Please write and explain to me how you feel, so I can help you—and everyone will leave us alone.*

"You two good over here?" Hannah had come up behind them. Fig turned to smile at her, and her cheeks flushed as she realized that Hannah was close enough for Fig to smell vanilla perfume. Sometimes perfume gave Fig headaches, but she didn't want Hannah to move away.

Fig, caught up in vanilla, couldn't find the words to say, so she was grateful when Danny chimed in. "We're okay!"

"Okay. And, hey, don't think I forgot about that overdue book fee," Hannah added.

Fig was about to defend herself, though by saying what she wasn't sure. But she caught sight of the mirth on Hannah's face, and blushed when Hannah winked. Like Fig and Danny, she must have come to the library straight from school. She was still wearing the Catholic high school uniform.

Fig liked the way Hannah rolled her skirt at the waist, and the way she wore her uniform shirt unbuttoned, displaying the light pink tank top underneath it. She liked Hannah's frizzy hair and her chipped nail polish. She liked Hannah, liked looking at Hannah, more than she had ever liked looking at another person. Hannah made Fig feel warm and made Fig blush. Fig knew what a crush was, even though she didn't know exactly what to do about it yet.

"Learn anything new about Mr. Gogh today?" Hannah asked.

"It's *Van* Gogh," Danny corrected her.

Fig nearly kicked him under the table.

"Well, what did we learn about Mr. *Van* Gogh today, then?" Hannah said, smirking.

"That he made way more art than Fig's dad makes music."

This time Fig *did* kick Danny.

Danny yelped just as Hannah said, "Your dad's a musician? That's so cool."

Fig felt her chest tighten as Hannah looked at her expectantly. "Yeah, he . . . he used to be. I mean, he still is. But he used to be more. Before."

"Before . . . ?" Hannah asked.

"Here, look," Danny interrupted, shoving his phone into Fig's and Hannah's faces.

Fig had to push the phone away to get a good look, but right there on Danny's screen, front and center, was a photo of her dad looking much younger. He was waving from a grand piano up on a stage, bathed in bright lights, with a smile even brighter on his face.

Fig had never seen him look so good.

Fig's chest felt even tighter, and she pushed the phone away. "I thought you were Googling Van Gogh, *not* my dad."

"But that's him, your dad—right?" Danny asked as he skimmed the article the photo was attached to.

"That's so cool," Hannah said, reaching out to grasp Danny's phone for a better look. "He must be awesome. This says he sold out Carnegie Hall. Have you been?"

"No," Fig said, though she wished she had. She ignored the way her nose burned as Hannah continued scrolling. "He hasn't played a show since I was a baby." She'd seen photographs in old dusty albums. She knew what he was before he had her. She wanted more than anything to witness that someday. "Stop Googling my dad, Danny."

"All right, all right," Danny said, taking his phone back from Hannah.

Hannah kept her gaze on Fig, and Fig wanted her to stop. She didn't want Hannah to know the things the other kids at school did.

"All right," Hannah said. "I have, like, a mountain of books to shelve before Mrs. Gregory gets on my case. I'll be over there if you need me."

Danny kept scrolling through links on his phone, and Fig couldn't tell if he was looking for information about her dad or Van Gogh. She closed the biography she was reading, eager to go home.

As Fig walked into her house, a strong smell immediately assaulted her nose, and she screwed up her face in alarm. "Dad?"

"In here!" he called from the kitchen, which didn't ease her concern.

She dropped her backpack and library books at the door and made her way down the hallway, stopping at the doorway to the kitchen and peering in. She had the urge to laugh and scoff all at once when she saw him standing at the stove. He was wearing a ratty and ridiculous-looking floral apron he must have found buried in a drawer. The sweat on his forehead made his hair stick up in odd directions as he wiped at it with one arm.

"What are you doing?" she asked.

He turned around to face her, his eyes a little wild even as he smiled and held up his spatula, twirling it in the air and getting some sort of sauce on the stove top and his apron (and the wall, really) in the process.

"What's it look like?" he asked. "I'm tired of takeout. I'm going to make us a proper meal."

Her dad did this sometimes, but those times were few and far between because he rarely had both the energy and desire to cook. In any case, his attempts in the kitchen always ended in a mess, even if it was a delicious one. Fig figured she would try to contain some of the chaos. "Can I help? What're you making?"

"Curry," he said. He dropped a kiss on the top of her head and made his way past her, then opened the refrigerator and pulled out some produce. "And no worries, I've got it."

The produce was fresh, and Fig was impressed and surprised. He had clearly gone shopping.

"There is something you can help me with, though," he said, his back to her as he cut up spinach and okra on the counter. She noticed that the back of his neck and ears were pink, but that could have been from the heat of the stove top. "All this trouble for a guest I don't even know for certain is coming."

Fig felt her stomach drop. "What guest?" She glanced at the calendar. There was nothing written in the white square for today, but CP&P could drop in at any moment. Did he know something she didn't? "What guest, Dad?"

He put down his knife and wiped again at his brow. "Can you dash across the street and invite Mark for dinner?"

She blinked at him. "What?"

"To, you know." He shrugged, focusing back on the curry. "Say thank you."

This was all for Mark, then. "We only have two chairs."

"Darling, please." He wiped a hand over his face, which was now clean-shaven thanks to Mark, because her dad could not do it and Fig could not do it, but Mark could. "I put us in danger and I just . . . We should thank him."

Fig almost said no. She almost said that Mark had seen enough and inviting him back for another visit was a mistake. That Mark stayed in the first place only because he thought her dad couldn't be left alone with her, and what, exactly, did her dad think about that?

But her dad had gone grocery shopping and was actually making dinner and was sweaty and trying, and Fig couldn't let him down. She put her shoes back on and made her way across the street to knock on the door of the yellow house, feeling her own cheeks grow a little warm even in the cool fall breeze. Mark had somehow experienced the intimate details of Fig and her dad's life but didn't call the police, didn't threaten her dad. The entire thing made her nervous.

The door opened. Mark stood there as he finished buttoning up a shirt, his hair a little damp. Fig figured he must have just washed up from work, which meant he probably hadn't yet started his own dinner. She didn't know if she was bummed or relieved. "Hi, Fig," he said, and then glanced behind her to the house across the street. "Everything okay?"

She took a deep breath, trying to ignore his assumption that things weren't okay. "We . . . I mean, my dad . . . He wondered if you'd like to come for dinner. To . . . say thanks."

Mark blinked, and Fig suddenly worried about what would happen if her dad went through all the trouble, all the mess and sweat and energy in their kitchen, only to have Mark reject them. But then Mark slowly smiled. "Yeah, sure," he said. "Of course."

"Cool, okay," Fig said, and exhaled deeply. "I'll tell Dad you're coming."

When, an hour later, Mark knocked on the front door, Fig was exhausted. Her dad was exhausting. Her dad cooking was exhausting. But at least, between the two of them, they managed to have dinner ready (with a couple of dad-daughter secrets about exactly how they got it ready). Fig had set the coffee table with napkins and utensils and plates for three.

"You're early," her dad said, basically accusing Mark while opening the door.

Mark shifted from one foot to the other. "Fig didn't tell me what time to come over. I can come back later?"

"Dad, let him in," Fig said from her seat on the couch.

"She's right," her dad said, and held the door open wider as Mark stepped aside. "Come in, come in. Just excuse the chaos, would you?"

As he walked in, Mark's face scrunched up, and Fig knew the feeling. She found herself laughing. "Dad burned the curry," she explained.

Her dad, still in his apron, with his hair sweat slicked, floundered a bit. "Don't worry, though!" he said to Mark. "I saved most of it. It's perfectly edible. I mean nice! It's nice!" He paused to take a breath. "Look, it's fine—I promise it doesn't taste like it smells in here, all right?"

Mark looked over at Fig before smiling at her dad. "Okay," he said.

Her dad ushered Mark to sit on the opposite end of the couch from Fig. "We've only got two chairs in the kitchen. We don't entertain a lot. I hope you don't mind."

Fig watched Mark carefully for his reaction, but he simply took his seat on the couch, as if it didn't bother him.

And then her dad was disappearing into the kitchen, leaving her and Mark alone. They both just sat there. Fig tried to avoid eye contact and wondered if it would be rude to pull over her dad's laptop and watch Netflix—she still was using Madison's log-in—but her dad's desperate "Fig!" from the kitchen saved her. She bounced up from her seat and left Mark to his own devices.

Fortunately, and surprisingly, it wasn't actually that long before dinner was served. While the smells and the state of the chef had been a little unnerving (for Mark, Fig imagined, as well as for her), her dad seemed to have pulled off dinner. They sat in the living room, plates on their laps, and Fig smiled as her dad presented their meal to Mark.

"Chicken *tikka masala*, *saag bhaji*—"

"That's curried spinach," Fig interrupted.

"Which is, yes, mostly spinach, and *bhindi bhaji*, which is okra, and honey rice." He smiled, and Fig smiled more, because he was blushing, but he also seemed so proud. "And there's more in the kitchen if you want seconds."

"Wow." Mark dug in, and Fig held her breath until he chewed and said it again, "Wow."

Her dad dug into his own plateful. Fig couldn't help it and started giggling, and he scowled at her a bit—because it was their secret for the moment—and then they were all eating.

Conversation was slow, and a little awkward, but then Mark finally asked the question that Fig was almost waiting for. "How'd you cook this okra so well? My mom used to serve it all the time, but I hated it then. It always ended up all slimy."

There was a moment of complete silence. Her dad looked like a rabbit caught in the headlights, and Fig tried her best to smother a laugh in her hand. He glared at her, then slouched back in his chair and surrendered to the moment. "Oh, fine, just tell him," he said with a put-upon look that didn't quite cover up his smile.

"He ruined dinner," Fig said between giggles as she let the secret out. "That's from the restaurant around the corner. They do really good okra."

Mark burst out laughing, even though he tamped it down as fast as he could, and her dad sighed. "My dear daughter does like to embarrass me," he said. "I did my best."

"I appreciate the effort," Mark replied.

Fig felt a little bad spilling her dad's secrets. "Dad spent practically all day cooking."

"Thank you, darling. I don't think Mark needs to know exactly how much of a prat I made of myself."

"I wish you'd told me," Mark said, setting his near-empty plate down on the coffee table. "You shouldn't have gone spending money on all this just to feed me."

"He swore like anything when the okra started getting all oozy."

"I didn't ruin everything, did I?" Her dad pouted, putting down his own plate, the food half eaten. "I had to rescue the curry—which I'll have you know," he said, turning to Mark, "I *did* make from scratch. And some of the side dishes sort of got away from me while I wasn't paying attention."

"So he sent me for extras," Fig added. "Otherwise, you'd be eating your *tikka masala* and *saag bhaji* with slimy okra and uncooked rice. But the curry and the spinach is all him."

Mark chuckled. "Well, they're both great. You shouldn't have gone to so much trouble, though."

Fig smiled at Mark for the compliments, even if her dad looked quite embarrassed. Her dad deserved them, and hearing them from a stranger (*was* Mark still a stranger?) was new. "I don't really cook a lot, except easy stuff for the two of us," her dad said with a shrug. "Seemed appropriate, though. Not every day someone saves your life, so a nice bit of food from back home felt right."

There was another moment of silence, then Fig said, "Dad, this is Indian food—you don't come from India."

Her dad looked up. "I'll have you know, young lady, this food was invented to get the British eating curry, and it worked like a treat."

Fig scoffed and argued that it still wasn't British, and her dad asked what she knew about being British, and Fig argued that he should just accept he was more American now than British. Now her dad scoffed, and Mark laughed, shaking his head at both of them as they all finished dinner.

Done eating, Fig excused herself to wash her hands and brush her teeth—mostly to avoid being wrangled into doing the dishes. She closed the bathroom door and looked at herself in the mirror, fogging it up as she inhaled and exhaled deeply. She couldn't remember the last time she saw her dad so . . . so happy and *normal* around someone that wasn't, well, her. She couldn't remember the last time she saw someone else so happy and normal around her dad, either.

Did that make Mark her dad's friend now? Could they trust him to be?

When she left the bathroom, she heard her dad at the kitchen sink, splashing and clanging, but she spotted Mark in the center of their living room, looking at the photographs along the walls. Fig hung back behind the doorway, hiding as she watched Mark's eyes move from photograph to photograph. Most of them were of Fig at various ages. Some of them included her dad—when he was young, and she was younger, and they were floundering but together.

Not a single photograph was more than eleven years old, as if time before Fig did not exist—hidden away instead in old photo albums—as if her dad wanted to pretend it never happened.

"She left," her dad's voice suddenly rang out, and Fig retreated a bit back down the hall to stay out of view. Her dad must have been watching Mark, too.

Mark looked over at him, his eyebrows creased together.

"See, I know what you're thinking," her dad said as he crossed the room to stand next to Mark. "There's a glaring omission here, so I'm saving you the trouble of asking. She left, just as soon as they'd let her."

It made Fig's stomach hurt that her dad didn't sound bitter or angry. He sounded like it was what it was, and, sometimes, even Fig believed that.

"She was just . . . done," he said.

Mark didn't respond, just kept looking at the wall of pictures, at Fig's first smile and first laugh and first step. "How old was Fig?" Mark finally asked.

"Less than a day," her dad replied. "She left Fig in the hospital, and I haven't seen or heard from her since. Called me up and told me I was on my own, she wasn't coming back. I got there as quick as I could, and the baby was just . . . alone, you know? And I held her and she was squirmy and waving her fists about, all angry, and I knew it would be the two of us from then on."

Mark looked horrified. Fig didn't blame him. There were so many unanswered questions. Why did she leave? Where was she now?

Would CP&P try to find her if they took Fig's dad away?

But Fig didn't want to hear the answers, and didn't want Mark to hear any more, either. "Dad?" she called out, letting her presence be known, knowing that her dad wouldn't continue that particular conversation with her standing there.

"You left me with the dishes," he said, softly accusing her, before bringing a hand up to cover a yawn.

Mark took that as his cue to leave. "I should get going."

Fig's shoulders sagged in relief. Her dad, his hair still a mess and his eyes droopy, looked drained. Maybe preparing a curry dinner, so close after the storm, was a little too ambitious. She loved him for trying and loved him even more for succeeding, but she was ready for Mark to go home just in case they were pushing their luck.

Her dad escorted Mark to the front door. The two of them stood there awkwardly, her dad small and leaning up against the doorframe, Mark much taller as he hovered over the threshold. "Thanks," Mark said. "It was . . . I had a fun evening."

"Me too," her dad said. "Thanks for coming. And thanks for, well . . ." He looked over at Fig, then back at Mark, and shrugged. Fig didn't blame him for not knowing the words to thank a new neighbor, practically a stranger, for braving a storm, for bringing him home, for staying with his daughter through the worst of it.

Mark shook his head and waved her dad's gratitude off as if it were nothing, even though Fig was certain they all knew it was definitely *something.*

They stood like that a second more, and then Mark was out the door, smiling and looking back to wave at Fig—who waved, too—and then he was walking away.

Her dad watched him go, watched until he knew Mark was safe behind the closed door of his yellow house.

# THE STARRY NIGHT

THINGS SHIFTED AFTER THAT THANK-YOU DINNER. Mark didn't go back across the street to the yellow house and stay there and keep to himself as Fig hoped he would, as Fig liked about Ms. Minkle. Instead, he came around more.

Mark usually got home from work around the same time Fig got home from school. Fig often found her dad across the street, helping Mark unload his truck filled with things like wooden planks and tools and concrete blocks. Her dad's fingers made music. Mark's made more practical things.

The first time Fig had arrived home to find her dad helping Mark unload the truck, she had been certain he was going to hurt himself. A couple of weeks later, she still wasn't exactly convinced he wasn't going to, but Mark seemed to have a handle on it. More times than not, Fig would get home to see Mark laughing and quickly grabbing the blocks or toolbox out of her dad's hands to carry them inside himself. Her dad wasn't really helping much, but Mark didn't seem to mind.

Which, again, was new. Which, again, made Fig wonder what Mark really thought about her dad.

Today, she walked toward her house after departing the school bus to find her dad chatting leisurely with Mark—and he never used to do *anything* leisurely—across the street. She hoisted the library book she was carrying higher on her hip, and picked up her step, eager to get home to join them.

Her dad's face was bright as he spotted her. "Fig! Look!" He was gesturing wildly at Mark. "Man with a tool belt!"

As it turned out, Mark was indeed wearing a tool belt, along with a sweatshirt (Fig thought she should probably find and wash the one her dad borrowed during the storm and give it back) coated lightly with dust. He was resting against his truck, the back of which was open, with large planks of smooth wood sticking out of it. "Don't be rude," Fig said. "I like it."

"Didn't say I didn't like it," her dad replied. "He just finished making someone a front porch."

"Fancy."

"I'd like a front porch, wouldn't you, Fig?"

Fig dramatically rolled her eyes for his benefit and turned to Mark. She didn't know what to make of Mark—or what he thought of *her*—but she offered him a shy smile. "Hi."

"Hey," he replied, and jutted his chin in the direction of her books. "Library again?"

At some point during her slight distraction, her dad crept up behind her and pulled the book right out from under her arm. "What's this? Mr. Van Gogh still? That art teacher of yours making you write his entire life history or something?"

"No, Dad. I told you."

"You did?"

"We have to paint for the Fall Festival. This one's a little hard to read. I needed to renew it so I can keep trying. We have to paint something, and Miss Williams gives us time at the end of every class to do it, and I *still* don't know what to paint. I'm hoping to figure that out soon, though. You said you'd come."

"Of course I did, darling. Of course I did." His voice was a little fast, and a little loud, and she wondered if he actually did remember. He flipped through the biography. "No more weather books, then?"

"That reminds me, I still need to pay the library for that book. Remember? I told you about that? They're not gonna let me take out any more books if I don't pay soon." Fig looked over at Mark, hesitant about bringing him into the conversation.

"Fig!" Her dad shouted her name so loudly both she and Mark jumped. "You've never seen *Starry Night*!"

"It's literally the first painting that comes up when you Google Van Gogh, Dad." She turned again to Mark, trying to read his expression at her dad's burst of energy.

"I don't mean photographs. I mean the real deal. At the MoMA! We should go." He thrust the book back to her, and she almost tumbled over at the sudden weight of it. "Go put your school things inside and wash up. We can get to the city before dinner."

Fig's mouth fell open. "You mean today? Right *now*?"

"Why not? Just a hop, skip, and a train ride over." He gestured wildly again at Mark. "How about you? You ever been to the Museum of Modern Art?"

Mark's eyebrows reached his hairline. "Ah, no."

"Good. Come with."

"Wait," Fig said, trying to bite back the smile that wouldn't stay off her face, trying to understand the situation, trying to make sure she wasn't getting this wrong. "We're really going to go? Right now, to the city?"

"Not if you don't hurry and change we won't. Do you have a friend you want to drag along?" He turned to Mark: "You go get ready, too. You're all dusty. No dust in the museum."

Fig could not picture Ava or Madison or Haley coming to the city with their camera phones and giggles and her and her dad. She thought, for a moment, about Danny. But then she shook her head. She wanted this all to herself. She had never been to an art museum. She'd never seen a painting up close before. To go see *The Starry Night*, in person, to see the colors and the thickness of the dried paint, to see the very work that Van Gogh touched with his paintbrushes and fingers during a time when his mind and his life were slowly falling apart . . . to see and experience and step into that world of art with her dad?

"Give me ten minutes, Dad!" she said, turning to run inside. "And don't you dare change your mind!"

Her dad was hyper and erratic. Fig sat with him and Mark on the train on their way to New York City to see one of Van Gogh's most popular paintings (not one of Fig's favorites, but the one that popped up in books and online most often) and tried to enjoy it. She was buzzing with the same nervous energy as her dad's; they were both unable to sit still. Her dad's leg bounced as he tapped his foot, while Fig constantly shifted in her seat to get a better view out the window. She wanted to show her dad the things she had learned, she wanted to experience this with him, and she wanted them both to understand it and each other.

Her dad wanted her to see *The Starry Night*, and they—and Mark—were going to.

Her dad was chatting away with Mark as if he actually had a friend in this world who wasn't his eleven-year-old daughter. Mark laughed at the things her dad said, not with malice, not at her dad's expense, but because he genuinely found them funny. In a short time, Mark had gone from new neighbor to almost a real friend, and Fig hoped nothing would happen between their home and the city and back again to change that.

Fig had a tight feeling in her chest. She kept thinking about how her dad could change his mind midroute and turn them around, or could get agitated and cause a scene resulting in a police escort home and a quicker follow-up visit from CP&P, or could do any number of things that could—and usually *would*, in Fig's experience—go wrong.

The train came to a stop, and her dad reached his arm out toward Fig and said, "Shall we, then?"

Fig almost asked if they could turn around. Instead, she took his hand.

Fig was nearly certain that, besides that first year of her life, she had never been to New York City, and it was confirmed when they stepped off the train and made their way out of Penn Station and she saw the not-so-starry night sky. Her eyes were wide as she looked up at the bright lights of the skyscrapers and billboards. These were the very lights she could see reflected across the bay at the shoreline by her house, the lights her dad sometimes stood at the edge of the ocean to stare at.

The city was a reminder in more ways than one how small she was, especially as people in suits pushed their way past her to get into the station, as people with cameras and smartphones bumped into her for a better view of the buildings and lights and life around her. Someone walking by gave her a shove, one that knocked her off balance, but a hand was suddenly there, firm and steady on her shoulder, keeping her in place. She glanced up at Mark, who looked slightly overwhelmed, too, but smiled at her in a way she thought was meant to be comforting.

"Fig? Fig!" Her dad was temporarily separated from the pair of them by a wall of tourists. Fig reached forward to again take hold of his hand. His palm was sweaty, but he held hers tightly, and Fig gave him what she hoped was a reassuring squeeze.

He seemed to calm slightly at the feel of her hand. Her dad looked from Fig to Mark and back, and he nodded, firmly and sure, signaling he was ready to move forward. "Right. Let's walk, shall we? Much easier than braving the transit at rush hour."

"You know where you're going?" Mark asked through the sounds of the city.

"Of course I do. Spent some of the best years of my life here. Only thing those years were missing was Fig."

Once they set off, Fig had no reason to worry about the decision to follow her dad's whims into the city. He kept his hand firmly wrapped around hers and walked them through those streets like a seasoned New Yorker, like someone who knew which streets were the less crowded ones, which sights Fig would like to see along the way. *There's Rockefeller Center. And that's Radio City. You've seen the Christmas commercials. Rockettes!* Fig felt safe as she marveled at the light that shone in her dad's eyes. He looked as happy as she was that they were there together.

And then, as they turned a corner, she saw it, those big black letters against white: *MoMA*.

Fig held her breath.

"You ready?" her dad asked.

She thought about everything she ever read about Van Gogh. She thought about the paintings she saw in all those books, about the project that had been weighing on her mind. She thought about her dad, the musician, the man who saw and heard things she didn't in music and art and the ocean and the clouds. She exhaled and nodded. She saw the crinkles at the corners of his eyes as he squeezed her hand.

The museum was as crowded as the city streets, and Fig stood exceptionally close to her dad, and even Mark, as they waited on line to purchase tickets. She sighed in relief when her dad pulled cash out of his wallet—she didn't want to deal with the possibility of a denied credit card—and sighed again when Mark insisted on paying for himself. They had walked the city streets, had physical tickets in their hands, and were finally waltzing through security and up an escalator that led to the galleries.

Nothing was going to keep them away. This was real and was happening.

"Where to?" her dad asked, looking at the signs on the wall. "Where would your Vincent be?"

Fig read enough to know that Van Gogh would be on the fifth floor with, according to the signs, the other painters from the 1880s through the 1950s. They could easily take the escalators to pass the other floors and get there quickly, but Fig didn't want anything about this trip to go by too fast.

"I want to see the other floors first," she said, knowing that her dad would love the artwork, and there was so much to see, and she didn't want to miss a second of it. "I want to see everything."

So up the escalator they went, to the second, third, and fourth floors, where her dad both critiqued and adored all the artwork. Fig didn't really understand much herself, which was frustrating, especially as her dad marveled with an artist's eye at pieces that made no sense to her. "What do you think of this one?" he said, pointing to a brightly colored painting of what looked like jumbled, disjointed bits and shapes thrown together.

It was called *Do the Dance* by an artist named Elizabeth Murray.

"No one's dancing," Fig said. She didn't even think any of the shapes were people, though really, she wasn't certain.

"I think it's a reference to a Ray Charles and Betty Carter song," her dad said because of course he knew that. He was the musician, the artist. Fig was just Fig.

At least Mark didn't seem to get it any more than she did, judging from the way his entire face pinched up, and as her dad went on and on about the paintings, it reminded Fig of those rare moments when he explained a musical piece. Fig greatly admired the way that part of his brain worked, but she wished she could unlock that same part in her own.

But then a painting did catch her eye, and Fig eagerly pointed to it. "It's a bedroom!" she said. The plaque under it said the painting was by Roy Lichtenstein, *Interior with Mobile*. "Van Gogh has a painting of a bedroom, too. The one from his yellow house. He painted it because he really wanted to start an artists' group where he moved to in France, and he was eager and excited to get other artists to come stay with him."

Her dad's eyes were bright and his smile wide as he listened to her. "You're better than a tour guide," he said.

Maybe Fig could do this, could understand, after all.

The rest of the journey went similarly, with her dad joking to Mark about the architecture: "Can you build me something like that?" And Mark commenting on Andy Warhol's soup cans: "My kitchen cabinet looks like that."

Fig loved it. She loved the MoMA, loved being there with her dad.

She thought that when they finally got to the fifth floor, they would walk into the gallery and see the painting, and her dad would turn to her and she would explain everything. She would explain the scene, the technique, the story behind it, and her dad would listen and understand and see the branches that connected Vincent van Gogh to the two of them. But when they finally reached *The Starry Night*—surrounded by a swarm of museumgoers holding up their cell phones and tablets for photographs and bumping against one another—Fig noticed that her dad was sweaty. He was wringing his hands, his eyes were slightly unfocused, and he was scanning the room and bouncing on the soles of his feet.

Her dad, who had been hyper ever since they left Keansburg, was not okay.

Mark noticed, too. "You want to go get some air real quick?"

"No, no." Her dad shook his head. "We're finally here! Have a look, Fig, go on."

Fig wasn't ready to take her eyes off her dad.

Mark placed a hand on her dad's back, not guiding, just suggesting, as he jutted his chin in the direction of the corner of the room. "We'll go look from over there. Less crowded. You want to squeeze your way through and then come meet us?" he said.

She looked to her dad (who looked relieved). He nodded and said, "Yeah, just . . . have a good look and then come meet us, right over there, right away."

This . . . wasn't how Fig planned it, and she felt her nose starting to burn. She wanted to take him by the hand and tell Mark to stay out of it and pull her dad through the crowds of people and their smartphones and stick him front and center and tell him, *Look, Dad, look at this painting that means so much to me because Vincent is so much like you, and I need to know both of you.*

But she couldn't. Not when he was standing there looking small and frail and tired, his fingers moving restlessly against his legs and a bead of sweat dripping down the side of his face. She acquiesced with a nod, and Mark patted her dad gently on the back, leading him to the less crowded space.

And then they were gone, and Fig turned to face the large crowd, alone, knowing that she was too small to see unless she managed her way to the front.

It took some patience, some clever maneuvering, and some ducking around cell phone cameras, but she finally stood—not quite front and center, but center enough—in front of Vincent van Gogh's artwork.

*This morning I saw the country from my window a long time before sunrise, with nothing but the morning star, which looked very big*, read the plaque on the wall next to the painting. Van Gogh had written the words in France in a letter to Theo, and Fig felt even smaller as she gazed up at the painting, seeing the brushstrokes, the thickness of the paint, the swirls and colors. She had to stop herself from reaching out to touch it, from running her fingers over those strokes, following the movement with her eyes instead. Her mind went to what she had read about Van Gogh. He'd been sitting in a mental hospital in Saint-Rémy, the bandage around his head covering his damaged ear, as he saw something only an artist could see and put it to paper for Fig to marvel at now while her dad waited at the back of the gallery, trying to keep himself together.

Fig's vision went blurry from tears. She blinked them away, and went to find Mark and her dad.

They were leaning up against the wall, exactly where they said they'd be, standing together, facing *The Starry Night*, and experiencing it without her. She pushed her way between them. "Was it special, love?" her dad asked.

"Yeah," she breathed, rubbing her fingers on her earlobe. Her dad was still sweaty, and she could tell by the way his fingers were fluttering against the sides of his jeans that they were shaking.

"Is your ear bothering you?" he asked.

She quickly dropped her hand because she wanted, *needed*, him to stay focused on the painting. She needed to keep him here with her, and not shaky from the crowds and lost in his head. She needed this moment to be like she imagined it. "Did you know it was Vincent van Gogh's brother who convinced him to use more colors in his work?"

"Oh yeah?" It was Mark who replied.

Fig tried not to frown. "Yeah. And I don't know if you can see from here, but he used this art technique called impasto, where he painted really thickly, so you can see the brushstrokes."

Her dad breathed a soft laugh. "Wow. All that reading is paying off, huh?"

She smiled and again blinked back tears. "And you see the tree, the dark part? That's a cypress tree. He painted those a lot because they have them in France, near the asylum where he lived for an entire year."

She caught Mark's eyes as they narrowed on her, and for a moment she blushed, wondering if he'd made the connection she had made from the beginning.

But it was her dad who spoke next. "There was a subway stop I used to end up at a lot back home in London. It was right about the time I was auditioning for schools. I'd get off, and you know, it's dark and windy and grimy in the Underground, but once I'd get up the stairs, the first thing I'd see was daylight and fig trees."

Fig had never heard this story before.

"Anyway, I was there so often, the daylight and fig trees started to feel like home. The familiar sight after coming up from the darkness. The music I wrote looking at those fig trees got me into the Academy."

Fig didn't know what to say to that, and the three of them fell into silence as they stood against the back wall, watching people taking pictures, chatting with friends, admiring the artwork.

"I'd like to hear you play sometime," Mark finally said.

Her dad let out a soft laugh. "Yeah. Sometime."

On the train ride home, Fig didn't say much to break the silence. She rested her head on her dad's lap, enjoying the sounds of her companions as they spoke softly with each other. She closed her eyes to picture the swirls and colors of *The Starry Night*.

Fig felt something when she looked at that painting, hung on its own wall at the MoMA, surrounded by people who wanted to see it, people who made her dad sweaty and nervous because there were too many of them and it was all too much for him. She felt something, too, as she stood in the back corner with Mark and her dad. *The Starry Night* was too far away for them to see the brushstrokes, maybe too far for her dad to see it at all. But Fig listened as he spoke about his own art, his music—the one thing that always made sense to him, even if it didn't always make sense to Fig. She listened as he told her about his fig trees.

And it all came to her in that moment, and she knew what she wanted to paint for the Fall Festival.

Fig closed her eyes and ignored the way her dad's leg frantically bounced under her head. Instead, she focused on the way the pads of his fingers played invisible tunes against her arm as the sun slipped lower and lower in the sky, and September finally came to an end, lulling her to sleep.

# October

*Fishermen know that the sea is*
*dangerous and the storm terrible,*
*but they have never found these dangers*
*sufficient to keep them ashore.*

—Vincent van Gogh to his brother Theo,
May 1882

# SORROW

FIG WAS AWOKEN BY THE SOUND OF SOMETHING SHATTERING, and everything she had tried to ignore and avoid the night before came crashing down with it.

She climbed out of bed, yanked open her bedroom door. Her dad was in the kitchen, murmuring and shouting things, and although his words didn't make sense, they didn't need to. Fig heard them loud and clear. He was confused, he was angry. Something hard hit the wall with a thud before falling to the floor. Whatever it was, he had thrown it. She swallowed thickly, took a deep breath, and braced herself. She had done this before.

She walked barefoot to the kitchen but didn't go in. She watched her dad pacing frantically, talking to himself, his eyes large and wild. Fig started tugging hard on her earlobe. "Dad? Dad, it's me. It's Fig."

He turned to look at her, and she shrank back at the expression on his face, the one he *never* directed at her unless he didn't know he was doing it. He wasn't here with her right now. She didn't know where he was. She didn't understand what happened to him when the dad she loved got trapped in that brilliant but terrible mind of his, and she hated it.

She hated that she never felt so far away, never felt so lost and unable to find him as she did in these moments.

"Please, Dad. It's me. You're okay. I'm right here."

But her words didn't register. He slammed his hands against his forehead as he closed his eyes and let out a cry that made her stomach hurt. She thought about the books she read, about the violent outbursts that led Van Gogh to cut off his ear, that made him eat his own paint and poison himself, that eventually ended his life.

Art and music didn't matter right now. Not to this version of her dad. She should have never let him take her to the city. She should have known better.

But that made her remember Mark, right across the street, the new neighbor-turned-something-more who shaved her dad's face, who helped him find a quiet corner in an overwhelming museum. She still didn't know if she could trust him. Right now, though, she didn't have any choice but to try.

Without another thought, without shoes, without a jacket, Fig ran out the front door and across the street.

She pounded on the door at the yellow house over and over and over again as she repeated in her head, *Please be home, please be home, please be home . . .*

The door swung open quickly, and with force. Mark stood there gaping at her, his shirt unbuttoned over his white T-shirt, his tool belt strewn alongside the door, and his shoes on but untied. It was as if he were about to start his day, not for one second expecting this interruption, not thinking about the crazy man and his daughter across the street. "Fig, what in God's name—"

"It's my dad—I need your help. I knew last night was . . . *Please*, you have to help!"

"What's wrong, where is he?" Mark stepped out of his home and closed the door behind him, and she wondered if he was ready to go pull her dad out of the Atlantic once again.

"Home, but he's not *him*, he's going to hurt himself. *Please*."

Mark crossed his lawn, and the street, and yanked open Fig's front door, and Fig could barely keep up with him. She stopped at the threshold of her home, not wanting to go in, wanting Mark to fix everything like he fixed porches, solve the problem as if it were as easy as finding a quiet corner in an otherwise loud and crowded room. She wanted to trust him to make things *better* for once, so she wouldn't have to do it herself, so she wouldn't have to wonder what might happen if she couldn't.

Her dad's hand was bleeding, blood from the side of his palm dripping down his forearm, and honestly, Fig expected worse.

But Mark wasn't used to this. He said to her dad, "You need to sit down, let me look at that."

Fig couldn't hear what her dad said, or maybe he didn't say anything that made sense anyway, but the tone was frenzied, his words hot in the thick, tense air in the room. Fig closed the front door and stood at the edge of the kitchen, watching as Mark grabbed at her dad's shoulders and used his foot to nudge a chair from under the table. "Sit down."

"Get off me, mate." Her dad shoved Mark, and Fig stepped back farther. If this went bad—if this went *really* bad—and Mark was here, Fig knew CP&P would come and take her away. She wanted to scream. She felt the wail in her throat, pushing out from the tightness in her chest as her earlobe started throbbing.

Her dad reached for the teakettle on the stove, and Fig closed her eyes tight, not wanting to see, not wanting to know what might happen next, just wanting it to be over.

But her dad did not throw the teakettle, because Mark started yelling. “Hey! Calm down right now and *take a damn seat*!”

His voice was loud, and it boomed in a different way from her dad’s. Fig’s eyes popped open and she took another step back. Her whole body shuddered as she watched Mark and her dad, head to head, practically nose to nose, standing off with each other. She wished she could take back the terrible choice that she made. She wished she’d never knocked on the yellow house door, that she hadn’t dragged Mark back into this.

But her dad didn’t yell back. His shoulders slumped, and Mark guided him to the chair, and he actually sat in it. “That’s it, buddy. Sit and breathe for a minute, and I’ll put that kettle on, okay?”

Her dad’s eyes were glassy, but he nodded. Still, Fig’s stomach kept hurting.

Mark filled the kettle with water and turned on a burner, and her dad remained in his chair, even as Mark crossed the room to Fig. "You get picked up by the bus, right?"

"What?"

"The school bus. You take the bus to school, right?"

He might as well have been speaking Russian. "I can't go to school today."

"Yes, you can. And you will. It's what he'd want, and he'll be fine. I'm staying right here all day, okay?"

Fig shook her head, fiercely. "No. I'm not going. I can't." There was always a chance her dad could get hurt, or CP&P could stop by without warning. It was the start of a new month, a fresh page of the calendar for them to drop by. "I need to be here."

"You got a phone?" Mark asked.

"What? Yeah."

"Give it here," he said, and she reached over to grab her backpack from by the door. Unzipping the front pocket, she pulled her cell phone out and handed it to him.

"I'm putting my number in," Mark said. "You call if you need anything. Or if you want to check in. How long until the bus comes?"

She glanced at the clock. "Like ten minutes. But I'm not leaving."

"You hurry and get dressed. I just need to make a phone call, and I'll be free to stay here all day. He won't be alone, okay? I'll be right here."

Fig didn't move. She searched Mark's eyes, trying to figure out what was happening. "You're staying?"

Mark nodded. "I just need to call out from work, and I'll stay here all day. Until you get home. Okay?"

She didn't want to leave, she really didn't, but she didn't want to stay, either. Her dad was hard sometimes. And Fig wasn't afraid, she *wasn't*, but still, sometimes . . .

Mark was here, and he had broken through her dad's fog when she couldn't. Her dad was sitting at the kitchen table, waiting silently for the water to boil. Fig would not have been able to calm him down like that.

But, still, this was bad, wasn't it? Mark kept seeing more and more of what went on in their house, and if anyone else knew what Mark now did . . . "Please don't call CP and P," Fig whispered.

Mark's eyes shot back to hers. "What?"

"Please don't call them," Fig said again. "He can't help it, and he's never hurt me, and he wouldn't have hurt you. He just gets confused. The CP and P people don't understand, and they can't see him like this before November thirtieth. *Please*."

Mark looked back toward where her dad was still sitting, slumped in his chair in the kitchen, before refocusing on Fig. "I'm only going to call work," he said. "That's all, okay? Your dad and I will sort this out."

The kettle started to whistle, and Mark went back to the kitchen. Fig hesitated for one last moment before going to her bedroom to change. She had two minutes to spare by the time she was ready to go. She popped her head back into the kitchen, just to look at her dad one more time, and she overheard Mark as he said softly, around sips of his tea, "We're going to figure this out, okay, Tim? We're going to sit here and talk and figure this out."

At school, Fig kept biting the inside of her cheek to keep from crying. She spent every class staring at the clock, watching the seconds and minutes and hours tick by, one leg bouncing under her desk. She wanted the school day to be over so she could get home and see—hopefully—that her dad's bad day was over, and they could just move on. New month, fresh start, blank calendar and canvas.

Across the classroom, Madison was leaning forward in her seat to whisper to Haley as Mrs. Beckett, the math teacher, began taking attendance. Early in the school year, Ava had chosen to sit in the desk next to Fig's because Fig was good at math and Ava wasn't. Now, Ava was writing notes in her notebook and holding it up when Mrs. Beckett wasn't looking, for only Madison and Haley to see. Ava kept her back turned to Fig, her long, tightly braided hair swinging lightly as she tried but failed to keep her giggles quiet.

Fig had her phone on her lap, just like Ava always did, but Ava used hers only for Snapchat. Fig, meanwhile, had Mark's number pulled up on the screen, just in case she needed it. Or in case he needed her. The girls kept laughing, and Mrs. Beckett yelled, "Settle down!" And all the while, Fig kept wondering, *Should I have really left Mark alone with my dad?*

"Hey! So I was thinking." Danny's voice was suddenly in her ear, startling Fig out of her thoughts and making her jump. He had swapped seats with Jaden Freeman. "I think we should set up your dad with Miss Williams."

Fig stared at him for a moment, certain she wasn't hearing correctly. "You think *what*?"

"Miss Williams lives alone. My mom is sometimes all 'She's too young and too pretty for that!' because she's nosy," Danny explained. "She goes to conferences with my teachers a lot."

"What? *Why?*" Fig asked.

Danny rolled his eyes. "My mom wants to make sure I'm adapting well, but she usually ends up just chatting with them anyway. Which is why I know Miss Williams is single."

"Quiet, Mr. Carter!" Mrs. Beckett called out from the front of the room. "Do I need to move your seat?"

"No," Danny mumbled, then added for only Fig's ears, "I don't even sit here."

Mrs. Beckett finished taking attendance, and she then told them all to take out their homework, which she would walk around the room to check. Fig pulled out her notebook, and—with Mrs. Beckett preoccupied checking the students' work—Danny leaned back over to whisper, "Miss Williams is an artist, so she would appreciate your dad as a musician."

"What would that help?" Fig asked. "And why would Miss Williams even want to date my dad? She's the reason we're in this mess to begin with."

Danny frowned. "She was trying to help. That day in art class—"

"I don't want to talk about it," Fig interrupted. "Besides, my dad has me. Vincent van Gogh only needed his brother. His love life was doomed, but he always had Theo. It's the same with me and my dad."

"Finola and Danny," Mrs. Beckett said, "do I need to repeat myself?"

"No," they both said. Fig slumped in her seat. She hated extra attention. Especially when Ava turned around to look at her.

"Have you thought more about Ava's party next weekend?" Danny whispered. "It's supposed to be a Halloween party, even though it's before Halloween, so you gotta wear a costume."

Mrs. Beckett came to check the homework in their row, so Fig didn't answer him. Instead, she looked over at Ava, who was writing notes to Haley again. Sometimes it felt like a different lifetime from when she might have been whispering and writing notes with them. They didn't seem to talk much about her dad anymore, but as they moved on from gossiping about him, they also moved on from her.

"Put your phone away," Mrs. Beckett said as she reached Fig's desk. Fig had forgotten it was still in her lap, had forgotten for a moment that Mark was home alone with her dad.

She slipped the phone into her backpack and looked back at the clock, the second hand ticking much too slowly for her liking.

Fig didn't know what she should expect when she got home. She had never left her dad with anyone else during an episode before, and while she wanted to believe Mark wouldn't lie and call CP&P on them, she barely knew him. He barely knew them. There were a million ways in which things could have gone wrong in the hours she was at school, and by the time the last bell rang, she knew this because she spent the rest of all her classes imagining each and every one.

The school bus doors slid open with that awful screech, and Fig started walking down the stairs, squinting in the bright sun, but then stopped in her tracks, nearly causing Mikey Ramirez to crash into her back. She stumbled to the side, out of the way, and continued gaping. Her dad and Mark stood there, waiting for her, as if this were a normal occurrence. She couldn't remember the last time her dad had met her at the bus stop, which was only up the street from their house. But there he was, his hands buried deep in his pockets (though she could still see the movement of his fingers tapping against his legs). He looked like he hadn't slept in a week, and he definitely hadn't shaved, but he was there, and he was whole. He smiled sheepishly at her, and she found herself running the short distance to him.

"How was school?" he asked, as if this were their regular routine.

She played along. "Fine."

He looked at Mark and back at her again. "I was hoping we could take a walk. There are some things we want to talk to you about."

*We?* Fig thought, looking at Mark.

Mark held out a hand to take her backpack from her, and she let him as her dad led them all down the road toward the shoreline. They walked quietly along the boardwalk, the sounds of the crashing waves their background music. She wanted to suggest they find a bench because her dad seemed so small, so jittery, but she followed his lead. She tugged at her earlobe, which had been sore all day, until another hand pulled hers away. She looked up to find Mark watching her, looking at her ear, but she shrugged him off. She couldn't help it lately, even if her ear was starting to hurt, and she didn't want Mark knowing that.

Finally her dad stopped walking. They faced the Atlantic view he loved so much and that right now made Fig feel so much smaller, so much farther away from him, and the kids at school, and Vincent van Gogh, and art, and everything.

Still, he said nothing.

"Are you feeling better, Dad?" Fig asked.

He chuckled softly. "I don't deserve you, Fig."

She glanced at Mark, and then back at her dad as the wind off the water picked up. Now October, the air was already colder than it was last month. Fig shivered, and her dad pulled off his favorite West Ham scarf and wrapped her up in its burgundy-and-blue stripes.

"Mark and I talked after you left." He paused, then laughed and shook his head. "Actually, Mark talked. I was rather belligerent."

That made Fig smile. "I'm shocked."

"Don't be cheeky," he said, then became serious again. "Anyway, long story short, we went through the referrals CP and P gave me and found a doctor, a regular one, who will see me and sort of, you know, help figure things out from there. Sort of like a checkup. I'll go chat with her, and she'll point me in the direction of what to do next."

Fig didn't like the sound of that. "A doctor? You've done that before, it just upset you. It made things worse. It was too hard and you couldn't afford it. *We* can't afford it."

"You don't worry about that." He looked over at Mark again, then back at her, and Fig felt strangely like a third wheel, the spare part, even though this was a conversation between her and her dad. "It's just . . . just to see," he continued. "To find out options. It's a start."

She shook her head. "Why can't *we* talk about this? Don't I get a say?"

"It's a good thing, Fig," Mark chimed in.

Fig shot him a glare. "He doesn't need a doctor. They won't understand, like Miss Williams didn't understand and CP and P doesn't understand. And what if they try to take you away from me, Dad—"

"That'll never happen."

"What happens then? Where would I go? Would they look for my mom?"

"*No*," he practically growled.

Fig didn't relent. "And what if it doesn't work? Vincent van Gogh got help, he went to doctors and a hospital and an asylum, and he still died. He shot himself and he *died*."

"I'm not Van Gogh, love."

"He didn't want to be sick, either. He checked *himself* into the asylum. It didn't work. No one understood him. He was scared of being sick, and he didn't get better and *he died*."

"But *I'm* sick!" His voice was loud on the empty boardwalk, and Fig stopped, tears dripping down her face. He reached out to wipe them away before continuing. "If I wasn't, social services wouldn't need to come back to check in on us. If I wasn't sick, your art teacher wouldn't have had to worry about you. But she was right to worry about you." He looked over again at Mark, who nodded, and then took a deep breath.

"I know we don't talk about . . . You asked me if I'm feeling better, yeah?" He stood in front of her, his hands reaching out but not yet touching her, his fingers trembling slightly. Fig nodded, and he continued, his fingers moving more against the air, playing music that, like always, was only in his head. "I feel . . . I feel like there is something vibrating inside me. I feel anxious and jittery and scared, Fig. And this is me when I do feel better. You do such a wonderful job of taking care of me, but we need help, both of us, because it can't be all on your little shoulders. And I need to stop feeling this way."

She looked out at the ocean, at the view in which her dad so often sought solace, trying to find whatever it was he saw in it that made him keep looking. Her nose began to burn as she fought back more tears. It was weird to be having this conversation after all these years in front of the very view that, because of her dad's mind, caused them so much trouble. Weirder still, with Mark standing there, too.

"As for your mum . . ." He paused and looked out toward the water. "She's not coming back, Fig. She gave up her right long ago."

"Where would I go, then?" Fig asked again.

"Right here. You'll stay right here," her dad said. "That's the point of all this. That's why the doctors. So we can make sure we both stay right here."

She tried again, fiddling with the frayed edges of her dad's scarf. "But Van Gogh—"

"Lived over a hundred bloody years ago," he interrupted. "Try and have a little faith that things have changed."

Fig said nothing.

"All right?" he prompted.

She paused, staring at the ocean. She didn't think any of this was all right.

"Okay," she breathed, and the three of them walked home.

# UNDERGROWTH

"That's beautiful, Fig." Miss Williams's smile was big and full of teeth and directed right at Fig. Fig averted her eyes to her paper.

"Thanks," she mumbled, her voice soft and cheeks warm.

"You should be ready to start painting soon. I can't wait to see it finished and to hang it at the festival," Miss Williams said. "Your dad is going to love it."

That made Fig look up into Miss Williams's eyes. Part of her wanted to yell at Miss Williams, to tell her not to talk about her dad, to tell her that she had made things harder for them, not easier. She wanted Miss Williams to know that Fig was angry with her for hurting her dad, and hurting her, and that no stupid painting was going to fix any of that, no matter how hard Fig tried.

The bigger part of Fig *did* try, though. She wanted to show Miss Williams that she was fine, that Miss Williams was wrong, that Fig could learn art and learn her dad, and they would both be all right.

But Fig also knew that she had told her dad about the Fall Festival more than once now, and still, she had no reason to believe he'd be able to make it, didn't know what version of her dad she would get even if he did. His doctor appointment was that afternoon, but even so, if Fig was being honest, she didn't trust his mind—only his heart. When push came to shove, the broken bits of his mind often won those battles.

Miss Williams placed a gentle hand on Fig's shoulder, and Fig felt her body grow stiff. "Keep up the good work, Fig," Miss Williams said, her smile fading.

As Miss Williams stepped aside to talk to the next student, Danny leaned over to talk to Fig. "Have you figured out how to set up your dad and Miss Williams yet? When my dad got a girlfriend, he became way happy way fast."

Thoughts of the festival, and doctors, and mental health made Fig's jaw clench. She didn't want to set up Miss Williams with her dad and didn't understand why

Danny kept pushing it. She nearly growled in response, "No. My dad doesn't need that." Vincent van Gogh needed only his brother. Fig's dad needed only *her*.

"All right, all right. But anyway, I was also thinking," Danny began, and Fig bit her tongue to keep from snapping at him, because of course he was. "If you want, maybe you can come over after the party tonight. If you can go, I mean."

Madison, from the other side of her, leaned over Fig's desk to get into the conversation. "You're going to the party tonight?" She sounded surprised.

That caught the attention of Ava, who was texting under her desk. "Who is? Fig?" she asked, then narrowed her eyes. "Who's taking you?"

"I am," Danny said, and Ava and Madison exchanged glances.

Fig blushed, gripped the edges of her desk. "Maybe. I mean, if that's okay?"

"My sister's got people coming over, too," Ava said. "So everyone will be there."

It wasn't really an invitation, but it wasn't a rejection, either, and it was much more than Fig had gotten from Ava in a long time. "Oh. Cool. Yeah, I mean. I have to ask . . ." Fig stopped herself from mentioning her dad. "I have to make sure, but I mean, it sounds fun."

"What are you going as?" Madison asked.

“I’m going as Wonder Woman,” Ava chimed in. “So I hope you weren’t planning on that.”

Fig shook her head. Her palms were starting to sweat against her desk. She hadn’t thought at all about what she would be, and now it was too late to think up anything good.

Danny was looking at her with his big eyes and gap-toothed smile, and Ava and Madison were watching her expectantly. Maybe, she thought, this could get her back where she was with them before. Her dad wouldn’t be alone, now that he had Mark right across the street, and plans to see doctors, and real plans to get better. (Plans that he made with Mark, and not her, but if he could make friends and make plans . . .)

Fig realized she really, really wanted to go to the party.

“Okay,” she told Danny. “Yeah, I’ll come.”

When Fig got home from school, Mark was outside her house, mowing the lawn. “Why’re you doing that?” she asked.

He wiped at his forehead and turned the mower off. “Just helping out. I have to do mine anyway.”

“Is my dad home?” She cut to the chase. “Did you two go to the doctor?”

Mark leaned up against the lawn mower and smiled at her. "We did. He's inside resting now. He was pretty exhausted when we got back. Try and let him sleep some, okay?"

"I always let him sleep when he needs to," Fig said with a slight frown. "What'd the doctor say? Is he going to be okay? Can they help him? What's going to happen?"

Mark glanced toward the front door before looking back at Fig. "Your dad wants to talk to you about all that, Fig. Let him rest, and he'll explain it all to you."

"You can't just tell me?"

Mark sighed. "It's really between you and your dad."

*If that was true, then he and I would be the ones to know, and you'd be on the outside.*

Fig tugged her earlobe. Mark reached forward to pull her hand away, but Fig flinched and pushed him away. "Don't touch me."

He froze, his hands in the air. "I'm sorry, I didn't mean to . . ." He stopped and took a deep breath. "What can I do to get you to trust me, Fig?"

She didn't know how to answer that. He had shaved her dad's face. He had helped at the museum. He stayed when her dad needed him, and helped him call doctors, and went with him to the appointments. He saved him from that storm.

Fig shrugged, slumping her shoulders as she looked down at her shoes. "I'm sorry."

Mark shook his head. "Don't be sorry."

She stood there with him for another moment. Fallen leaves blew around the lawn along with the newly cut grass blades. The crisp air caused Fig to shiver. Mark kept looking at her, and she almost—*almost*—told him everything. About how much she hated CP&P and the random drug tests, and how mad she was at Miss Williams. About her art project that she finally started and wanted, more than anything, her dad to see. About how the kids at school were finally, maybe, treating her normal again. About how sometimes she wished her dad were more like Mark because sometimes she just wanted to be able to depend on somebody.

Instead, as she stood there, watching him in his work boots and gloves, with the sweat dripping down his forehead in the crisp fall air, Fig got an idea.

"You can start by letting me borrow your tool belt."

The house was quiet when Fig went inside. The sound of Mark's lawn mower echoed from outside, where he was back to work on his own lawn after lending Fig some of his things. Her dad's bedroom door was closed, and the house was dark, and she knew he was still sleeping. She pulled out her phone to text Danny, asking for the details. Once he responded, she rummaged for a piece of paper and a pen to write them all down, in case her dad was still sleeping when Danny's mom came to pick her up.

*Dad*, she wrote, and then hesitated. She closed her eyes for a moment and imagined she was Vincent and Theo van Gogh, writing letters, telling each other how they felt, all their worries and fears and feelings. She liked to think she and her dad were as close, that they were all each other had and the only ones who understood each other, but she hadn't felt so sure in a while. *Dad*, she wanted to write. *I'm trying so hard to be what you need, but I don't know what that is, and I don't know what I need, either. Sometimes I worry that maybe Miss Williams and CP&P might be right, and I don't know what happens if that's true.*

Sometimes, though, Vincent's brother got angry. Sometimes Vincent asked too much. Sometimes it was too hard for Theo to balance his own life with taking care of Vincent's. Theo had his own job, and his own wife, and eventually his own baby. Making sure Vincent was supported was sometimes too hard, sometimes too painful.

Sometimes Fig thought she could relate to Theo just as much as her dad could relate to Vincent.

So, instead of pouring out her heart, she wrote Ava's address and a note saying that she had gone to Ava's party with her friend Danny.

Her dad didn't come out of his room, so she left the note on the kitchen table when Danny's mom picked her up and drove them to Ava's. Fig wore Mark's tool belt (though he had taken out most of the tools) along with a pair of his safety goggles. She wore the pair of tan construction boots she got for Christmas two years ago, a little small but still manageable, and a flannel top over a white shirt.

Danny was dressed as a cop, and when Fig climbed into the back seat, his mom made a YMCA joke that Fig didn't understand. Danny rolled his eyes.

Danny's mom pulled up to Ava's house, which was on the other side of the highway from where Fig lived, the side that had bigger houses with backyards and fences and pools. Orange fairy lights were hung along the perimeter of the house, the bushes were covered with cotton webs, and a large spider made out of black garbage bags sat on the front lawn.

Before Danny could climb out of the car, his mom called after him, "Hey, you know the rules!"

"Yeah, yeah," he said, waving her off.

"I'll pick you two up later."

Fig waved goodbye to Danny's mom and walked next to him up the driveway toward the Washingtons' front door. "What are the rules?" Fig asked.

"No drinking, no drugs, and if there are either of those things or no parents, I better call her back here, or she'll kill me."

Fig laughed but then thought about what he said. "Is there usually drinking or drugs?"

Danny shrugged. "Depends who shows up, but I wouldn't touch it anyway." He reached for his fake gun holster. "I'm a cop." They both laughed at that.

Everyone liked Ava's parties the best. Her house had a finished basement with soundproof walls because Ava's brother played the drums, and that's where she had the parties. Her parents were home, but they didn't come down, and the kids never went up, so it was like having no parents there at all. Ava's mom answered the door and directed Fig and Danny to the basement. As they made their way down the stairs (the bannister was also covered with cotton webbing), they were immediately welcomed by Ed Sheeran singing loudly through the speakers, and the sounds of laughter and gossip and drums. The room itself was huge: carpeted, with couches, a wide-screen TV on one wall, and a foosball table that was being used as an actual table, with red plastic cups and chip bowls placed between and on top of the rows of little soccer players. The room was dark; the only light came from more orange fairy lights hanging from the ceiling. Kids were scattered throughout, in separate clumps based on age and friendships. Ava's sister, an eighth grader, had her own friends at the party. With the older kids in the mix, Ava's parties were supposed to be much cooler than anyone else's, although Fig noticed the eighth graders seemed to be keeping to themselves.

Fig felt out of her element and stood a little closer to Danny. Maybe this wasn't such a good idea.

But then Madison, wearing all black and cat ears, her nose painted black and with whiskers extending across her cheeks, was tugging on Fig's shirtsleeve. "Come get in our picture," she said. Haley (also a cop, like Danny, except a much prettier—although less practical—one in a skirt and heels) was holding her phone up trying to fit everyone in the camera screen. Fig found herself a little dazed as she let Madison pull her over, and she smiled into Haley's phone, and Lorde took over for Ed Sheeran on the speakers, and Haley was asking her what her Snapchat name was.

"I don't have—" Fig paused, then lied instead. "I dropped my phone and it shattered, so I've just got this stupid flip phone right now."

Haley laughed. "Well, once you get a new phone, add me on Snapchat."

Fig said that she would.

Once she settled in, Fig actually enjoyed the party. She talked with Madison about their art projects and complained about Mrs. Beckett with Haley, Ava, and a few of the boys. Some of the older boys snuck in cans of Bud Light, and Ava's older sister told them that they'd better not leave any behind when they left. When the music turned to a slow song, half the kids groaned, even as the other half paired off and pulled each other close to kiss and dance. "You should ask Danny Carter to dance," Madison said.

"What?" Fig asked.

Ava laughed. "You've been hanging out with him a lot lately. He's always following you around. He definitely likes you."

"Definitely," Madison agreed.

"He's my friend," Fig said, adjusting her tool belt to try and get more comfortable. "That's all."

"Oh, just ask him," Ava said, shrugging. "He's kind of cute, even if he's pretty weird."

Her words made Fig's stomach hurt. They had called her dad weird, too.

And Fig had agreed with them.

"Hey!" Danny said, making his way over to the group, and the other girls all immediately started giggling. "What?" he said.

Madison bumped Fig's shoulder, and she stumbled closer to Danny and found herself saying, "Do you want to dance with me?"

Danny's face lit up, his gap-toothed smile big and bright.

But just as he reached to take her hand, the basement door opened. "Fig?" Ava's mom called down.

"Fig! Fig, are you here?" Another voice rang out, panicked and recognizable, and Fig felt the music pounding in her ears, felt all the eyes in that basement seeking her out as she watched her dad take the basement stairs two at a time. Someone turned the music off.

*"Fig!"* His eyes were wild, and Fig could barely breathe as she had flashbacks to art class, to the way her classmates stared, to the moment CP&P showed up later. And now—just as everyone was starting to forget and no longer asking questions, just as things were feeling sort of normal at school—she heard snickers and accusations as the kids all pulled apart from one another, hiding beer cans under the couches and in pockets. Ava's parents stood at the top of the stairs, watching, as Fig's dad stood in the basement, in the private sanctuary of her classmates, in tears.

Fig wanted to scream at him. How could he do this to her again?

"Whoa, what's wrong with him?" one of the older boys said, and a few others laughed, and Fig realized this time was even worse. This was clearly not okay, and everyone could see now the difference between *weird* and *crazy*, and it hurt her to think it, because he was sick—but he was also ruining everything.

"It's okay, Fig," Danny was saying, reaching to grasp her shoulder, but she shrugged him off. She quickly crossed to her dad, pushing him back toward the stairs, hard, and Ava's mom and dad were both there, helping her get him up them. His hand got tangled in webbing, and he ripped it off the bannister while repeating her name, and Fig started yelling, "Just go, Dad! Get out of here!"

Fig closed the basement door behind them once they reached the top, shutting out the sounds of her friends and classmates and the party, but she continued pushing at him. "Why are you here?" she shouted. "How could you do this?"

Her dad was shaking and clinging to her, and Ava's parents were trying to calm him down and asking what they should do. (Was he okay? Should they call someone to come help? Did he usually get like this?) And Fig felt sick because the police were one phone call away,

CP&P was one phone call away. *How can he keep doing this to me?*

"Let's go home, Fig," her dad was saying. "Please, come home now."

*He doesn't mean it*, she tried to tell herself. *He can't help it, he can't help it, he can't help it.* She kept shoving him away from her anyway.

He reached for the goggles still on her face.

"Maybe we should call the police," Ava's mom was saying, and Fig thought she might throw up.

"No!" she shouted, yanking off the goggles. "No," she repeated more calmly. "I know who to call."

Mark came almost immediately. He thanked Ava's parents, promised them he would take care of things from here, and led Fig's dad out the front door. Fig followed them.

She waited, holding her dad's sweaty hand tightly as Mark moved her dad's car from where it was haphazardly parked in the street. She tried not to think about that—about what it meant to have him be this dazed and still driving.

"We'll get it tomorrow," Mark said as he took her dad by the shoulders to lead him to Mark's truck. Fig felt forgotten, her hand cold without her dad's to hold, until Mark opened the backseat door and motioned for her to hop in.

Mark drove them home, her dad up front in the passenger side of the truck with his head pressed against the window, eyes closed. His occasional murmurings and the way he kept lightly banging his head against the door let them know he was still awake, just not fully there. Fig sat behind Mark, trying to keep her gaze out her own window and away from her dad, though she kept meeting Mark's eyes as he watched her in the rearview mirror.

They hit a pothole in the road, and her dad banged his head against the window. Mark placed a hand on her dad's shoulder. "We're almost home, buddy," he said, and then looked back again at Fig. "You okay?"

"What did the doctor say?" Fig asked.

Mark focused back on the road. "Your dad wants to talk to you about that, Fig."

"Look at him!" Fig shouted, which startled Mark but didn't affect her dad. "He *can't* talk to me about it! He can show up and embarrass me and ruin Ava's party and ruin my life, but he can't explain to me *why*!"

Fig kicked at the back of her dad's seat.

"Don't do that," Mark said.

"Did he tell you that the lady from CP and P showed up at our door because my teacher called them after he did this, *exactly this*, to me at school? That when she came inside, he was *just like this* and could barely get off the couch to talk to her, so she mostly talked to me, and I didn't know what to say, and I must have said something wrong because she said she'd have to come back, and she's going to come back and she'll come back sooner if he keeps doing this to me!" She kicked the back of her dad's seat again.

"Fig, stop."

"You weren't there the first time he went out in a storm! I was! I had to call the cops and they came and that's why CP and P started a file on us! Ava's parents were going to call them again and they can't see him like this!"

"I know that!" Mark shouted, which stunned Fig into silence for a moment. Mark took a deep breath.

Mark's radio wasn't on, and their shouts echoed throughout the truck. The only other sounds were the wind as it hit the windows, the other cars on the road, and Fig's heavy breathing. Mark's grip on the steering wheel was strong, his knuckles turning white. "I know," he said more gently, and some of the tension eased from his shoulders. "You'd have been proud of him today."

Fig exhaled deeply, leaning back against the seat and wiping angrily at the tears that fell down her cheeks.

Mark looked over at Fig's dad, even as he spoke to Fig. "He didn't panic or shut down. He was honest with the doc, and she was real good with him. She isn't a specialist, but she obviously knew how to deal with someone who was having a tough time being there."

"But can they make him stop being like this?" Fig asked. "Can they help him?"

Mark adjusted his hands on the steering wheel, stretching out his fingers. "She thinks so. We'll talk about it more with your dad when he can, okay? But she thinks it sounds like some kind of bipolar disorder."

Fig slumped back in the seat. Vincent van Gogh, people thought, might have been bipolar, too.

"Are you okay, Fig?" Mark asked once more.

She nodded out of habit, but Mark's gaze met hers again in the mirror and she stopped. Mark gave her a smile. It didn't quite reach his eyes.

"Thank you," Fig all but whispered. It was a relief to have someone to depend on, to have someone to call besides the police. "For coming to get us."

"I'm glad you called," he said as her dad shifted in his seat, blinking at Mark as if he had just woken up from a long night's sleep.

Mark put a hand on her dad's shoulder and squeezed. "We're almost home," he said again, but whether to her or her dad, Fig wasn't sure.

Fig found her dad the next morning, awake and sitting on the living room couch, waiting for her. "Come sit down, Fig," he said, but she opted to stay where she was standing. "Mark told me you two talked."

Fig slowly nodded. "What does it mean, exactly?" she asked. "To be bipolar."

He ran his hands over his unshaven face. "It's like . . . Look, this is all new to me, too, sweetheart. But it's like how I'm all everything or nothing, you know? Two extremes. That's all it means." He held out his hand for her to hold, but she ignored it. "My brain doesn't do in between, and it's not healthy to be bouncing to and fro."

"I don't understand."

"Sometimes I'm depressed. And sometimes I'm manic. Do you know what that means?"

"Sometimes you stay in bed all day, and sometimes you . . ." Fig paused to take a deep breath. "Sometimes you ruin Ava's party."

He patted the spot on the couch next to him. "Come sit with me."

She wanted to. She wanted to curl into his lap and force him to make promises she knew he might never keep. Still, she didn't move.

"You know," he said, "you really shouldn't have left last night without talking to me first. I didn't know where you were. You can't just . . . leave a note."

"You weren't waking up!" she said, raising her voice. "You never wake up. You just fall asleep and leave me alone and I wanted to go to the party!"

He sank back a bit into the couch, looking down at where his fingers were folded in his lap. Fig gave in and went to him, sitting down beside him, leg to leg. He wrapped an arm around her, and she resisted the urge to rest her head against him. "I don't want to do that to you anymore," he said. "I want to be wide awake for you."

She was quiet for a moment, trying to fight back the urge to cry. "Can they . . ." she finally managed. "Can they treat it? The bipolar."

"Might take a while to figure out. But . . . yeah," he said. "They can treat it."

"Please don't do that to me again," Fig said.

"I won't. I'm sorry. I'm so, so sorry."

He reached for her hand, but she moved it out of reach. "They'll take you away, Dad. And I'll . . ." *I'll let them* was on the tip of her tongue, and the thought made her feel sick.

She swallowed the words back down. “I just want everything to be better,” she said.

“Me too, darling,” he replied. “And I swear to you I’m trying.”

Later that day, Fig found herself back at the library, approaching the front desk, trying to contain the heat that spread over her cheeks as Hannah stopped clicking away at the desktop keyboard in front of her and looked up to smile at Fig.

“Hey, it’s the Van Gogh girl again,” she said. “You have my money yet?”

Fig shook her head, cringing. “I’m working on it. I promise,” she said.

Hannah didn’t miss a beat, leaning in conspiratorially in a way that made Fig wish she could tell Hannah all her secrets, that Hannah would one day want to confide all hers in Fig. “So,” she said, “are we going to illegally check you out another book about Van Gogh today?”

Fig tried to be brave.

“I was hoping you could help me find books on mental illness,” Fig said. “About being bipolar.”

Hannah's fingers now rested on the keyboard. "Is this still about Van Gogh?"

Fig hesitated. Sometimes she went to sleep dreaming about going to the library and Hannah waiting for her with a tower of Van Gogh books on the table. Sometimes she dreamed that Hannah would come to the Fall Festival, and that Hannah would see Fig's painting and wink at her with that wink Fig loved and say, "Guess all my help at the library was worth it."

Fig did not picture her dad in any of these dreams, even if she wanted him at the festival, too. There was no stress in the ones Hannah turned up in. There was too much stress when she thought about her dad.

So she lied. She didn't want Hannah to know anything about him. "Yes. It's about Van Gogh."

"All right," Hannah said, already typing. "Let me see if we can find you something that's not too bogged down in science and academics."

"No, don't do that," Fig said. "I want the truest and best book you can find."

# 11

## THE SOWER

THE FIRST TIME FIG EVER EXPERIENCED DÉJÀ VU WAS that Monday, when she walked into class and every student stopped talking and turned to stare at her in silence. She had experienced this very same thing before.

So—like she had in September—Fig did her best to pretend it was coincidence as she took a seat at her desk. It almost worked. The others almost started talking among themselves again, Fig forgotten, *again*, but then Jeremy leaned over to loudly ask, "Hey Fig! How's your dad?"

Another hush fell over the room, and Fig wished Miss Williams would walk through the door. The silence was followed by a couple of gasps and giggles that her classmates could not stifle. Fig looked over at Ava because it was her party Fig's dad had ruined, but Ava would not look at Fig, would not make eye contact with anything but the phone in her lap.

No. This wasn't déjà vu. This was worse.

"Don't be a jerk, Jeremy," Danny said, diverting the eyes in the classroom to him. "Her dad's sick."

Jeremy shrugged. "I was just asking."

"No you weren't," Danny said.

Fig thought she might burst into flames and melt into her desk. She reached for Danny's arm, pulling him to sit down. "Don't. It's fine," she said.

Danny looked like he might argue, but Miss Williams finally walked into the room, and all the other students in the class shut their mouths and turned forward in their seats, as if they were good students, as if everything were fine.

Miss Williams noticed. "You're all unusually quiet today. Let's see if we can keep this up. Come get your papers and let's get to work."

Just like that, the moment was gone, and the class moved on. Fig didn't know what was worse. She wished she knew how to explain. She wished she knew how to apologize to Ava. But most of all, she wished one of them would say, *Hey, Fig, that sucks about your dad, but do you want to come to the next party anyway?*

No one did. They moved on with art class like normal, and Fig, instead of focusing on them, focused on the artwork. Next to her, Danny was working on a very bright rendition of what he was calling *Sunny Day*, which was his reverse version of Van Gogh's *Starry Night*. It wasn't a view of Saint-Rémy but a view of Danny's own backyard, with bright skies and colorful swirls of clouds and sunlight.

Fig loved it.

Her own work was going slowly, especially since Miss Williams gave them only the very beginning or very end of class time to work on their pieces. But Danny offered insights that he learned from his art classes at the library, and Miss Williams suggested different uses of colors and showed her how to get her proportions right. Fig was dubious she would ever be a real artist, at least not like Danny or her dad, but she was starting to feel much better about her work. She wanted it to be good; she needed it to be.

The bell rang, and Fig and her fellow students began gathering their things and putting away their paints to head to their next class. Fig was the last to leave, and Danny was waiting for her in the hallway. "Is your dad okay?" he asked. The question sounded much nicer coming from Danny than it did from Jeremy.

"He's . . . He'll be . . . I'm sorry I had to leave you alone at the party." She sighed. "I have to get to gym."

"Hang on, Fig, I don't care about that." Danny grasped her shoulder to keep her from leaving. "Wait, I want to ask you something."

They both just stood there silently for a long moment as Fig waited for him to do so. Fig tightened her hold on her backpack. "What is it?" she asked as students pushed around them to get where they needed to be.

"We've been hanging out a lot. And I really like talking about art and stuff with you," he said. "And, well, I really like you, too."

Fig shrugged. "I like you, too."

He smiled, all teeth and the gap front and center. "Oh, good! Because I was wondering if you would be my girlfriend."

The late bell rang. Fig stood still, staring at Danny.

When she said nothing, his smile started to fade. "I mean, I just . . . I thought we had fun together and stuff," he said. "You asked me to dance."

"We do, I did," Fig said. "But, I mean . . . you're my best friend."

"Best friends can be more than best friends."

Fig nodded. She did believe that was true. But Danny didn't know about the way she thought about Hannah. "I think we should just be best friends."

Danny was frowning now, in a way that looked like he couldn't control it, even though he tried, the corners of his mouth pulling down of their own accord. "But . . . why?"

She didn't know how to explain, but she didn't want to lie to him, either. "I'm sorry, Danny. I can't be your girlfriend."

He didn't argue with her, didn't try to persuade her or change her mind. He nodded, once, slowly, and backed away from her, both of them already late for class and headed in opposite directions.

When Fig got home, she found her dad sitting at his piano, in the nook off the side of their living room, cast in shadows. He wasn't playing—his hands weren't even on the keys—and Fig walked over to flip on a light so he wasn't draped in darkness.

He turned and blinked at her.

"Everything okay, Dad?" she asked.

He said nothing for a moment but then slowly smiled a smile that looked more like a cringe, gazing past her toward the front door. "Can you get Mark for me, love? Please?"

Fig frowned, but her dad turned back to the piano, staring at the keys. She sighed and crossed the room to glance out the window. Mark's truck wasn't in the driveway. "I don't think he's home," she said.

"He's not home?"

"His truck's not there."

Her dad nodded, but the gesture was sluggish, along with the rest of his movements, and Fig went back to him. Mark wasn't here, but she was, and she wanted him to know that. "What's wrong, Dad? I can help."

To her relief, he smiled at her—a small but real smile—and patted the empty spot next to him on the bench. Fig quickly sat beside him, and when he placed his hands on the piano keys, she placed hers on top of his. "I'm feeling a little foggy today," he said, and pressed down on the keys. Fig's fingers moved with his to play a single chord. "I think it's the pills the doctor's having me try. Haven't been able to do much all day. Can't play a thing."

He pressed down on the keys again, playing that same chord.

Fig frowned. "I thought the medicine was supposed to help?"

"It is," her dad said. "It will. It's . . . not really an exact science. It just might take some time."

She pulled her hands off his and tugged at her earlobe. The ear ached as she touched it, but she couldn't stop. "I wish it didn't have to."

"Me too." He perked up for a moment, and Fig thought that maybe she was helping after all. "I almost forgot. I got you something," he said, and reached under the piano bench for a box she hadn't realized was there.

"What is it?" she asked as he handed it to her. The box was small and white, and her eyes opened wide and shot up to meet his as she realized what it was.

Her dad scratched at the back of his head. "Well, I just . . . I know you said everyone else had one. And I'm just . . . I'm so sorry that I make things so much worse for you in school." He shrugged. "After everything, I thought you deserved it."

She opened the box and held her new shiny and white and clean smartphone gently in her hands. She almost couldn't believe it. She wanted to turn it on immediately, and set it up, and download all the apps that everyone else already had, and text Danny and . . .

Her chest squeezed. She almost forgot.

Her dad squinted at her. "Why do you look so morose? I thought you'd be ecstatic."

"It's not that. This is great, Dad. Thank you." He waited for her to continue. "Danny asked me to be his girlfriend today."

Her dad scowled. On another day, she might have laughed at him. "Who exactly is this Danny? What are his intentions? Eleven-year-old boy, can't be good ones."

"Dad, come on."

"I'm serious!"

"I turned him down, so you have nothing to worry about."

He hummed a soft acknowledgment. Fig set her smartphone down on the top of the piano before running her fingers along the white keys that she never wanted to play but were so important to her dad.

"Why do I think that's not the end of this story?" he asked.

"Danny is my best friend. I feel bad."

"If he's your so-called best friend, I'm sure he'll understand, then."

She pulled her hands off the piano. "I couldn't figure out how to tell him why."

Her dad scoffed. "You listen here, Finola, boys do not need reasons why—they only need to hear *no* and that's that, you got me?"

He meant business when he used her real name, and Fig smiled because things felt so normal for a moment. "I know, Dad. It's just . . . I have a reason. And I want to explain it to him, but I don't know how." She paused, keeping her eyes downcast. She didn't want to ruin that feeling of normal. "I don't know how to explain it to you, either."

"You can tell me anything. You know that, right?"

This was different, wasn't it? This was one more thing that they wouldn't understand about each other. It was deep and personal, and meant something to her. Even if she couldn't exactly pinpoint what it meant yet. It was as much a part of her as his mind was a part of him. It was just Fig. She didn't know how to admit that to her dad, the man who was ready to threaten eleven-year-old boys on her behalf.

"I like someone else," she said, her eyes still on the piano keys. "Someone who isn't Danny."

"Aye, aye," her dad said. "Go on, then. Who is he?"

Fig sighed and looked her dad in the eyes. They were gentle, and soft, and wrinkled at the corners from age and past smiles and past everythings. "Her name is Hannah. She works at the library."

His eyes grew wider, but he otherwise didn't move.

"Okay?" Fig asked.

"Okay? Fig, love . . ." He paused, shook his head. "I'm going to mess up this conversation—you know that, right? So just . . . bear with me, for a moment."

She nodded, her fingers reaching again for her earlobe as she watched his eyes drift to the side for a moment before moving back to look directly into hers.

"So . . . you like girls, then?"

"I like Hannah," Fig said. "I don't know the rest."

He nodded. "Okay. And what . . . what exactly do you like about this Hannah?"

"Dad . . ."

"I'm just trying to follow."

"Well, what did you like about my mom?" she asked.

"She was drop-dead gorgeous in a dress, for starters."

It was the most he had ever said about her mom other than her leaving, and it was simple, and sort of silly, but somehow it gave Fig the courage to say more. "I really like Hannah's smile."

"Then I bet," he said, sliding an arm around her shoulders, "she has a very lovely smile."

Fig leaned into his embrace. "So . . . okay?" she asked again.

He kissed the top of her head. "More than okay."

# PORTRAIT OF THEO VAN GOGH

FIG WASN'T USED TO COMING HOME FROM SCHOOL and finding her dad in the middle of a piano lesson, but when she walked through the front door, dropping her backpack, he was sitting in his piano nook with Molly. They were caught up in a song and didn't hear Fig come in.

"That's it!" her dad exclaimed as Molly played, her fingers dancing on the keys just as gracefully as his. Fig always loved watching her dad play, and she kept quiet where she stood. She enjoyed watching Molly play, too.

The song came to a stop, and Molly was the first to notice Fig standing there. "Oh! Hello again!"

Her dad smiled at Fig, and Fig smiled back at both of them. "I didn't mean to interrupt. I'll just go do my homework in my room."

"Oh, don't!" Molly said, turning to face Fig's dad. "Can she stay?"

"That's up to Fig," he said. "By the way, Molly here is a mathlete! See, I told you. Music and math. Same part of the brain."

Molly laughed. "It's just math club."

"Let me go grab a snack," Fig said. She crossed the room to enter the kitchen and was startled by the pot on the stove top and the timer ticking away on the oven. "Dad? Are you cooking something?" she called.

"Just getting dinner started," her dad called back, and then the music started again as he and Molly resumed their lesson.

Fig checked the pot to make sure it wasn't boiling over and opened the oven to make sure nothing was turning black and crispy inside. But everything seemed normal, and the kitchen wasn't even that much of a mess. There were dirty spoons and bowls in the sink, and the stove top could use a good scrubbing, but it seemed that her dad had started dinner without much chaos.

Which wasn't really normal. At least not for them, and it almost made her nervous. He really cooked only when he was . . . What was the word the doctor used? *Manic*. But the kitchen wasn't a mess, and he seemed pretty calm as he played away with Molly, and whatever he was making actually smelled pretty good.

Fig walked back out to the living room, taking a seat on the couch in view of the piano nook. Molly stopped playing and turned to her, pushing her bright blue glasses back up her freckled nose. "Do you play, Fig?"

Her dad laughed. "Finish this song, and then I'll allow you to accost my daughter with all the questions you want."

Fig watched them as they practiced, nearly forgetting that she had her own homework to do. Molly was good—was *great*—and her dad was always more capable of taming a piano than he ever was of taming himself, and together the music they made almost lulled Fig into an afternoon nap. When the lesson came to an end, the silence that settled over the house was a stark contrast, and Fig was disappointed. She almost asked her dad not to stop.

"All right, I'll leave you with Fig while I cross-check the calendar with some of my last-minute appointments so we can make sure we're set for your next lesson," her dad said. He grabbed the calendar off the wall and took it with him as he headed for the kitchen. Mark had scrawled her dad's doctor appointments on a pad of paper on the kitchen counter. Fig thought it would be easier if he just wrote them on the calendar in the first place, but no one had asked *her* for her opinion.

Once he was gone, Molly popped off the piano bench to join Fig in the living room, immediately asking questions. "Do you go to Bolger Middle School?" Fig nodded, and Molly continued, "I go to Thorne. What grade are you in?"

"Sixth. You?"

"Seventh." Molly motioned at the piano keys. "So, do you play?"

Fig shook her head.

"I'm the only one in my family who does. My older sister quit, like, five years ago," Molly said, rolling her eyes. "And then my dad is an engineer, and my mom works at the bank right around the corner from my school. Both are why I'm in the math club. They're both also very boring."

Fig tried to imagine what that must be like. "I think," she softly admitted, "that boring can be pretty good."

Her dad came back into the room carrying the calendar he pulled off the wall. "Okay," he said. "I have an appointment next Wednesday. Ask your mom if Thursday would work instead."

“I will,” Molly said, and then her phone buzzed in her pocket. She pulled it out to look at it. “That’s her now. Thanks again for the lesson, Mr. Arnold!”

He walked Molly to the front door. “See you next week, hopefully.”

“Bye, Fig!” Molly called as she left.

Fig’s dad closed the front door behind her, and then turned to face Fig. “Want to help me finish dinner? It’s just chicken and pasta, so it’s not exactly all that exciting.”

Fig smiled. Boring could be pretty good, indeed.

It wasn’t until Fig was in bed that night, long after Molly left—and dinner was eaten—that she realized her dad had taken the calendar off the wall, flipped through the pages, and Fig had not thought about the circled CP&P date at all. She hadn’t once thought about hurricane season.

She slept very soundly all through the night.

Mark was becoming a regular fixture in their household, just like the third chair that magically appeared one day in the kitchen when Fig got home from school.

It was easier for Fig to count the days of the week that Mark *didn’t* show up for dinner as she continued to cross off more and more October boxes on the calendar.

Most of the nights that he did, her dad would send Fig for a shower, telling her to get into her pajamas, and when she'd come back into the living room, clean and ready for bed, Mark would still be there. He'd be on the couch with her dad, laughing as he tried to get her dad into football, and her dad tried to get Mark to understand music.

Her dad still did not care for American football, and Mark still did not understand music, but Mark did understand which pills her dad was supposed to take in the morning, which ones at night, which ones with food. Fig watched—not knowing any of it—as Mark filled her dad a glass of water at dinner to wash the pills down.

Fig wanted to be the one who knew what pills were which. She wanted to be the one who knew how to take care of her dad, but she was slowly becoming relieved that they had Mark, too, ever since he picked them up from Ava's. November was getting closer, along with the date on the calendar with *CP&P* written large and circled in pen. There hadn't been any more big storms since September, but the end of hurricane season was still over a month away. All of it was easier to worry about with Mark there.

Tonight, Fig padded barefoot back into the living room, her hair wet and pajamas comfy, and was greeted by the sounds of her dad's piano. He played a tune she'd heard only bits of before that sounded a lot more polished now. Mark was sitting on the couch, listening with a sort of calm serenity her dad hadn't experienced from an audience—even an audience of one—for quite some time. "Giving Mark a free concert?" she asked.

He kept playing, but his face lit up at the sound of her voice. "He does so love a free gig."

Mark shook his head with a laugh. "How about you, Fig? You ever play?"

Fig held up her hands. "Little fingers," she said.

"That's an excuse," her dad chimed in. "This one's too stubborn to have ever practiced. She can 'Heart-and-Soul' with the best of them, though. Come here, let's show him."

Fig sighed dramatically for his benefit but joined her dad on the bench. "I want the high part," she said, and that was the only cue he needed to start.

It was ridiculous, she thought, for this classically trained, brilliant composer to be playing such a jolly, simple tune with his eleven-year-old daughter, especially since his fingers still moved on the easy chords as if he were performing in front of a music hall audience and not just Mark. But the notes of "Heart and Soul" were quickly joined with the sound of their laughter, and Fig managed to get through almost the entire song without messing up.

Mark applauded when they stopped.

"Oh, don't egg him on," she said.

"Not egging," Mark said. "That was great. You two should see yourselves when you play together."

"You should have seen my dad back in the day."

Her dad scoffed. "You weren't even born yet."

"I've seen pictures."

"Pictures?" Mark inquired.

"Don't you dare," her dad warned, but Fig was already bouncing off the piano bench and jogging over to the cabinet in the corner of the living room. She opened a drawer to pull out an old photo album and wiped at it. The cover wasn't dusty, not really. She had flipped through it so many times before.

"He doesn't want to see those, Fig, stop that."

"Sure I do," Mark said, and Fig jumped up next to him on the couch, putting the heavy photo album on his lap and flipping open the cover.

The photographs weren't labeled, but Fig had made her dad tell her which concert hall was which, how many people were in each audience, what songs he performed, how he felt during each and every performance. As she flipped through the pages, showing them to Mark, they didn't need any explanation. They were photographs of her dad from a different time, one before her, a version of her dad that she sometimes couldn't connect with the person she knew. His hair was trimmed short, his face smooth and clean-shaven, with a bright, confident look in his eyes. But Fig sometimes still *could* see the dad that she knew in those pictures—still could see the way his smile sometimes didn't quite reach his eyes, and that those eyes sometimes had that sheen of exhaustion. Either way, it didn't take an expert to see that man had been, and still was, a talented pianist.

It didn't matter if he was playing in front of a crowd of fifty or two thousand and fifty. Even from those photographs, she could see how he commanded each hall; she could see how handsome he looked while doing so. She wanted Mark to see it, too. Wanted him to know that her dad was someone who had been, and should still be, taken seriously in his craft.

She wished there were some way to make CP&P see her dad as the man in these photographs instead of the man he'd been at that first visit. As she looked at him now, his face smooth and shaven and his eyes bright as he sat at his piano, she thought that maybe that was possible.

Mark was quiet as they flipped through the album, and when they reached the end, he started right back from the beginning again. "You clean up good," he said to her dad.

Fig's dad was pink around his ears and stayed in the safety of his piano nook.

"Women must've been throwing themselves at you." Mark had a smirk on his face as he said it, and her dad laughed, the blush spreading from his ears to his cheeks.

"Not likely," he said.

Fig leaned in. "My mom was a groupie," she confided.

"She was not! Don't go spreading lies."

Mark barked a laugh. "Well, I bet she wasn't the only one."

There was something about the way he said it that made Fig ask, "How about you? Did you ever have a . . ." She paused, unsure of how to refer to the relationship between her mother and dad. "Were you ever married?"

"Fig," her dad warned.

"It's okay," Mark told him. "Yeah, I was. She passed away about six years ago."

Fig frowned. "I'm sorry."

He shrugged. "Yeah, me too. But I've made peace with it, try not to have any regrets." He stopped, and his eyes drifted off to the side. "You'd have liked her."

"Yeah?"

Mark laughed. "She would have loved you, too. You're just like her. Fiery. Small and sassy. Kate kept me on my toes, never let me take myself too seriously. Made me promise to live my life and be happy."

Fig looked back down at the photo album spread across her and Mark's laps, tracing the shape of her dad's face in one of the photos with her fingers. She let herself, only for a second, think about what life would feel like if she actually lost him. "Are you?" she asked Mark. "Happy, I mean."

Mark took a deep breath, smiled at her, and then looked across the room at her dad. "Yeah. Or at least, I'm something really close to it."

"All right, Little Miss Nosy," her dad said, standing up from the piano bench. "Time for you to get to bed."

Fig drifted off to sleep that night to a lullaby of the soft murmurs and laughter from Mark and her dad, accompanied by his piano. The last image in her mind was of her dad in his best suit up on a stage, performing as if he were the best musician in the world—and she spent the night dreaming of orchestras and happiness.

It wasn't long after (nights like that had started to become so commonplace and comfortable, Fig forgot to cross days off the calendar) that Fig thought she was still dreaming of her dad's music until she blinked open her eyes and realized she was awake. The music was real and new and drifting through their house and her bedroom—at six in the morning on a Saturday, though she couldn't bring herself to care. She held her breath, listening to her dad's piano along with the tick of the clock in her bedroom, anxious to see how long this piece would last, how long until it spun out of control or abruptly ended or turned into something else, some other half bit of music he couldn't hold on to.

But it kept going. It grew stronger. It flowed, and it all came together, and Fig *loved* it. It was like being at the MoMA, looking at *The Starry Night*. It was like being there in the audience in those photographs of her dad's performances. It was the exact feeling she wanted to put on paper in Miss Williams's class. It was the very thing she *knew* would convince CP&P to leave them alone.

It was her dad, at his best, and when the music came to a stop it wasn't because he ran out of steam, or forgot the notes, or because his fingers didn't want to work anymore. It was because the song was *finished*. She hadn't heard him finish anything in years.

Could she get him to play it when someone from CP&P next came? Could she get whoever it was to understand how wonderful he could be?

Fig waited until she heard the shower running and climbed out of her bed, slowly opening the bedroom door to pad across to the nook where her dad's piano lived. She wanted to see it. She wanted to see his handwritten notes of sheet music, wanted to touch those sheets and feel that the music was real, wanted to familiarize herself with it, wanted to know it and be a part of it. She wanted to know that his life *before* her and *after* her could be the same.

The sheet music sat on top of the piano, and even before she got up close to it, she could see it was different. She could see how clean the sheets looked; there were no wrinkles, hardly any cross-outs or rewrites or big black smudges covering half the lines. It wasn't perfect—he had clearly been working on it for quite some time to get it just right—but it looked . . . professional. It looked like the kind of work she knew he was capable of, and this was *it*. This was what they needed. This was what he had to show and play for the next CP&P visit to prove the science wasn't exact, but it was *working* and his mind was fine.

She reached out so she could feel the piece in her hands and look at it, as if she understood music and could read it like a library book. But she froze, her hand in midair, the moment she saw its title, in her dad's scrawl, top and center: *MARK*.

Suddenly her dad's piano nook seemed a little too small for comfort. She stared, bewildered, at that piece of sheet music, Mark's name clearly legible in capital letters at the top. The last time her dad wrote anything in someone's name was the piece called "Finola" that he kept safe in his desk drawer. He hadn't finished anything since, hadn't been able to, and what, exactly, did this mean? Mark was his friend, and yes, he had helped them, had pulled her dad from a storm, but this seemed different, this seemed . . .

The shower turned off. Fig was stunned by the silence, a stark contrast to the music that had filled the house when she awoke. She quickly made her way back to her bedroom and closed the door. The notes of that song floated around in her head along with her confusion, and she made the decision to pretend she hadn't seen the new music if her dad said anything about it at all.

Danny was avoiding Fig. He switched his seat back with Jeremy in art class, and back with Jaden in math, and he sat with the rest of the boys in the cafeteria at lunch. Fig sat by Ava, Madison, and Haley, who swapped snacks and stories around her. She was once again fading into the background. Ava wasn't even looking at her these days.

But when Jeremy got sick in the middle of lunch (and all over the boys' table), his mom came and picked him up, leaving an empty seat between Danny and Fig in art class. Fig kept glancing over at him as he dipped his paintbrush in yellow, dragging thick swirls of paint along his paper.

She bit her lip, and took a chance. "So, my dad actually finished a piece of music."

Danny paused but kept his eyes on his artwork. "Really?"

"You won't believe what he called it."

Danny didn't respond, still didn't look up from his painting.

Fig kept trying. "I don't really know what it means, though. Maybe you can help figure it out?"

He cringed a little, and she almost thought he might apologize for all the time he wasted ignoring her. But he still wouldn't look at her, and he shifted his painting a little farther from her, so that he had to turn away from her to paint it. "I need to focus. Okay?" he said.

She nodded, even though it wasn't okay at all. They spent the rest of art class working in silence.

Fig rode the bus home silently, too. She told her dad she was going to go to the library after school, but now . . . now she didn't much feel like it. She didn't want to see Hannah. She didn't want to make excuses again for overdue book fees, and her feelings for Hannah were messing up her friendship with Danny. She just wanted to go home and see her dad, and ask him what to do, and sit with him on the couch and forget about everything else.

But he wasn't alone when she walked through the front door (which wasn't the weird part, not these days). What made her freeze at the threshold—her eyes wide, the fingers of one hand wrapping so tight around her backpack strap that the buckle dug into her skin, the fingers of the other hand reaching for her earlobe—was how she found him, found *them*.

Her dad and Mark: sitting close on the very middle of the couch. Mark's arm was around her dad's shoulders, and her dad's hand was resting on Mark's cheek, and they were looking at each other as if no one else were in the world, as if Fig weren't anywhere in their orbit, as if she weren't standing *right there*. They leaned closer and closer to each other, until Mark finally caught sight of her out of the corner of his eye, finally registered that she existed, that she was there. He pulled away from her dad, inhaling sharply. "Fig . . ."

Her dad's head whipped around, and he stumbled off the couch, nearly losing his balance as he turned to face her, his eyes frantic. He almost looked like he did on the days when his mind was useless and lost to him, and she almost wished it were true and he wasn't himself right now because that at least would explain this, would explain why she wasn't expecting this. She wanted to blame this on some manic episode, but she remembered that sheet music. She remembered his newly finished song, Mark's name centered at the top of it. And she knew he was clear, knew this wasn't a trick of his mind or hers.

"Fig, love. We can talk about this, okay?"

It wasn't okay. She didn't know how to explain that to him. Was this happening in the background of all those nights they spent with Mark, those dinners the three of them shared, the laughter over TV shows and sports games and music? Was this there during the conversations and secrets she confided in her dad, the ones in which she explained Hannah, without knowing he understood better than she knew, he understood and could relate to a part of her and didn't tell her, didn't try to be there for her the way she had been trying to be there for him with art?

She closed her eyes and tried to find the words to ask questions, to find out exactly what she saw, to get them to tell her the truth, but she couldn't say anything.

"Fig, please . . ."

And then she didn't want to say anything, and didn't want to hear any more, either. She didn't want to know.

She ran down the hallway and into her bedroom, and she knew her dad and Mark were both following her, her dad's hands on the door before she could slam it in his face. "Fig, wait, please. I'm sorry we didn't tell you. But I promise you, nothing has to change."

The words finally came, bursting out from her chest and up her throat. "*Everything* has changed!" Didn't he see that? Didn't he see the way she took an art class to be closer to him, even though she really loved science? That taking that art class for him was what put CP&P at their door? That it was because of her and Miss Williams that he was drug tested and checked in on? Didn't he understand that she spent Friday nights with him instead of with girls like Madison and Ava and Haley because they wouldn't invite her anymore, that her smartphone was useless because no one ever texted her anyway? That she read book after book after book about hurricanes, about Vincent van Gogh, about bipolar disorder, about mental health, and paintings and art and music?

Didn't he see how she tried so hard to be what he needed and see things like he did, and all this time he was seeing and experiencing those things not with her but with *Mark*?

"Mark is a good man. I care about him, and he cares about me, and we didn't want you to find out this way but—"

"No," she practically growled. "You can't do this!"

Maybe it was the way she was yelling at him, refusing to listen when he was trying to explain, but he squared his shoulders. "I'm sorry, darling, but you don't get to dictate my life."

Which only made Fig fight harder.

"You dictate mine!" she shouted at him. "It's because of you I don't have friends and can't go to parties, because *I'm* your Theo! I've always taken care of you—I'm the *only one* who knows how to take care of you, and it *sucks*, Dad!"

Mark stepped forward. "Fig, I'm just trying to—"

"You stay out of this!"

*"Finola."*

She paused, taken aback by the way her dad barked her real name. She took a deep breath through her nose, but still her voice cracked as she asked, "Why didn't you tell me?"

Her dad looked small. "I didn't know how."

That wasn't good enough. Not for her, not right then. "You're going to scare him off and make him leave us just like you made my mom leave us and you make *every-one* leave us!"

And that was a direct hit. Which was exactly what she wanted, wasn't it? Her dad was hard to live with, and it took a special person to live with him, but her mom couldn't do it, and Fig didn't know anymore if she could do it, and what would happen when Mark realized he couldn't do it, either?

Her dad's hands hung at his sides, shoulders slumped, his face crumpling as he looked at her.

"I'd never, Fig," Mark said, but Fig didn't want to talk to him, didn't want to see her dad's face look so sad and broken over something she said, didn't want to deal with this anymore.

"Get out of my room," she said, her voice going small and unthreatening. She didn't have anything left in her to yell. "Just get out of my room."

Mark turned to leave first, without hesitation, simply because she told him to. Her dad wasn't as quick to go. "I love you, Fig."

She didn't ask him to double it. He turned and left, closing the door, giving her the space she so desperately needed to breathe again.

# 13

# THREE SUNFLOWERS IN A VASE

FIG DIDN'T LEAVE HER ROOM FOR THE REST OF THE night, and come morning, her stomach was growling loudly enough she was positive that was what woke her up. It also could have been the fact that the entire house smelled like butter, or the clang and clatter she heard coming from the kitchen.

Fig wanted to eat but didn't know what to say to her dad. She took her time in her bedroom, putting on a skirt, a shirt, a cardigan, and socks, taking the time to tie and double-knot both her shoes and also run a brush through her hair. She quietly made her way into the bathroom she and her dad shared, where his toothbrush was haphazardly placed beside the sink. She moved it to sit in the holder, ignoring the medication case that Mark bought for her dad so he wouldn't lose track of the days of the week and the meds to take each day. She took her own toothbrush and brushed her teeth, washed her face. All these tasks didn't normally take her this long, but today she decided to take her time with them.

When Fig finally set foot in the kitchen, her dad was standing there in his apron, holding a plate filled with pancakes, as if now that they were made he didn't know what to do with them. "I made pancakes," he said, stating the obvious. "No chocolate chips, I'm afraid."

"Syrup?" she asked.

He cringed. "None of that, either. Jam?"

"Ew."

"I'm sorry."

She shrugged, taking a seat at the table. He took that as his cue to put the plate stacked with way too many pancakes in front of her and sat in the other chair. For a moment, they just sat there, him looking at his hands and her at her pancakes.

He asked, "Can we talk?" at the same time she said, "Will you braid my hair?"

He sighed, deep and heavy, as some of the tension left his shoulders. "Of course, love. Of course."

Fig gave him the hairband that was wrapped around her wrist, and he gathered her long dark hair into his fingers, scratching lightly at her scalp. His fingers danced around her hair, not quite as gifted as when they moved over the piano keys, but soothing enough to lull her eyes closed. She waited for him to speak, but he didn't, just kept to his task. When he finished, he tied the end with the band and rested his fingers gently on the back of her neck.

"Thanks," she mumbled. "I should go get my bus."

"Can I . . ." he said, suddenly and quickly, as she stood to gather her things. "Can I drive you to school?"

There was a part of her, and maybe there always would be, that wanted to jump into his arms and say, *Yes, yes please drive me to school, and come to the Fall Festival, and make me breakfast and dinner and tell me what you're feeling and about your illness and medications and please don't leave me, ever.* But right now, there was a larger part of her, one she didn't even fully understand, that wouldn't let her. "It's okay. I don't mind the bus."

He nodded and offered her a smile she didn't believe. "I'll see you later, then."

"Yeah," she said, and stood to head toward the door.

Her dad stood, too. She watched as he walked over to the calendar and crossed off the date. "October's going fast," he said.

Fig didn't respond.

"Fig?" he called as she put on her backpack. "Mark's going to come around for dinner. I just . . . I wanted you to know."

She paused, fought against the sudden urge to yell, and nodded instead. She reached for the doorknob. "Make something easier than curry this time," she said.

That got her a more believable smile. "You've got yourself a deal."

Fig quickly left after that, not giving him time to say *I love you* because she couldn't *not* say it back, not when it still was true. But, in that moment, she didn't want to.

At school that day, Fig kept to herself and her own thoughts until the bell was ringing at the end of fifth period, and Miss Williams was asking her to stay behind. "I'll write you a late pass, just hang back a second."

She didn't move from her seat as the other students put away their paints, stored their paintings, and filed out of the room into the hall, with the gossip and chatter echoing throughout the art room. Miss Williams closed the door, muffling the sounds from the hall, and Fig's stomach started to hurt. It was strange, being in the art room by herself, surrounded by other students' drawings and paintings and sculptures. The last time she was alone with Miss Williams was the day her dad burst into the room.

Miss Williams sat in Danny's old seat next to her, and she slid Fig's painting closer to get a better view. "It's coming along, Fig. You should be very proud of your work."

Fig shrugged. "Thanks."

"Do you want to tell me about it?"

"The painting?"

"Or about what's bothering you."

Fig's eyes shot up to Miss Williams's eyes, which were gentle and kind as they looked back, just like always. Miss Williams had the same crinkles at the corners of her eyes that Fig's dad's did. It made her wonder about the things that made Miss Williams laugh, and the things that made her worry, that put those crinkles there. "You didn't pick up your paintbrush all class," Miss Williams said. "And I know you and Danny haven't really been speaking."

"It's about my dad."

"Your painting?"

Fig shrugged again.

Miss Williams shifted the painting to look at it even more closely. "I understand that you don't trust me very much right now, Fig."

Fig's nose started to burn. "Did you know my dad braided my hair this morning?" She started speaking really quickly. "And he once wrote a song he named after me. He . . . he calls me Fig because he used to see fig trees outside the subway when he lived in London, and he wrote about them, too."

"Is that why you painted this?" Miss Williams asked.

"No. I mean, yes, but that's not what I mean," Fig said. "He's a good dad, Miss Williams. I know you don't think so and I know it's hard to tell because he's sick, but he's getting better. He's trying, and *I'm* trying, and I need you to believe me."

"I do believe you, Fig."

"No you don't. You want him taken away from me."

"That's not what I want at all." Miss Williams placed a hand on Fig's arm and leaned closer, her expression serious. "I'm sorry things are hard for you. I'm sorry I had to be the one to make that call. And I can ask your dad in for a conference, and the three of us can sit down and talk about it if that's what you need. But I need you to be safe, Fig. And your dad might be a great dad, but sometimes people need help. Especially if they're sick. That's all I wanted to do for you."

Fig rubbed her earlobe. Maybe that was true, but she couldn't help but wonder what would happen if he passed all his tests, if he took all his medications and listened to his doctors, if he got better and she painted a beautiful painting but still lost him anyway.

Fig stopped by the library after school. Her book was due, and the last thing she needed was another late fee. She saw Hannah at the counter, with her skirt rolled at the waist and a bright green tank top under her unbuttoned shirt, but Fig put the book in the return bin by the library entrance and walked back out without approaching her. Everything, right now, was too confusing.

Fig went right into her bedroom to do her homework when she got home, and when there was a knock at the door a couple of hours later, she ignored it. Mark was her dad's guest, so her dad could answer it. She would mind her own business until dinner was done, and then she'd eat, and she'd retreat to her room—and that would be that.

She heard the front door open, heard the muffled voices through her door. She wondered if they kissed each other in greeting, before immediately deciding she didn't want to wonder that at all. Fig made a mistake on her math work, and ripped out and crumpled up the page from her notebook. She had been starting to trust Mark, and she always trusted her dad, but neither of them seemed to trust *her* with much of anything.

When had that changed? When had Mark figured out the pieces of her dad that she was never able to?

"Fig! Dinner!"

Fig and Mark sat at the table as her dad scooped out the stir-fry right from the pan and onto their plates, then put it back on top of the stove and pulled out his own chair. Fig suddenly hated the addition of that third chair.

"Dig in," her dad said. "I even did the shopping today. Fresh veggies!"

He seemed so proud of himself, and Mark smiled at him, and Fig replied, in a way that dared him to think he didn't need her: "You left the stove on."

The goofy smile that was on his face slowly disappeared as he blinked at her, and it was Mark who was up and out of his chair to turn the stove off, moving the pan away as the rest of her dad's stir-fry sizzled and burned from the heat.

And Fig felt bad because she had seen that look on her dad's face before—the one that meant he tried so hard and failed anyway, and the world beat down hard on him for it—but she very rarely was the one to cause that look. Still, she didn't feel much like eating. Especially when Mark took a big bite and said, "It's very good, Tim."

Fig put her fork down.

"Don't be like that," her dad said. "Eat."

"No," she said, even though she couldn't remember the last time she was outright belligerent, and she folded her arms in front of her chest. Her dad's gaze flickered at Mark, before squaring away with hers.

His face was stern as they stared at each other, and she was bracing for him to start yelling, when suddenly he was flicking his fork back and food was flying into her hair. "What's wrong with you!" she squealed as she tried to duck out of the way of his stir-fry. She pulled a piece of green pepper out of her braid.

A bubble of laughter suddenly burst out of her dad, sounding a little uncertain but also uncontrollable. Fig wasn't sure what he found so funny. She snuck a glance at Mark, who looked as baffled as she was.

Her dad was laughing so hard he had to take a couple of deep breaths to compose himself. "Your face!" he managed between spurts of laughter.

She scowled at him and picked up her own fork. "Grow up, Dad," she said as she flung meat at his head.

"Don't! Don't," he said, still laughing, reaching across to grasp her wrist and prevent an actual food fight from breaking out. A piece of chicken slid down his hair and got stuck behind his ear, and then Fig, too, began laughing.

They were the kind of giggles that she couldn't control, and they were full of nerves and made her stomach hurt, but her dad kept laughing with her, wiping at the tears that formed in his eyes. Eventually even Mark joined in, although he didn't seem sure he knew what they found so funny.

The laughter slowly came to a stop, and the mood seemed to sober up as they settled. It was as if they had remembered where they were, and that their food was getting cold, and that her dad made such a nice meal only because he wanted to have a dinner with his daughter and his . . . his what, Fig didn't know. But she still didn't like it, still felt hurt and confused and betrayed.

"We didn't plan this, Fig," her dad said. "Not me, not Mark. And I can't . . . I can't explain it. And I know you must have questions and I know you're so angry with me, but I never went into any of this wanting to hurt you."

That much she knew was true.

When they finished eating, her dad declared that since he cooked the meal, he was not about to also do the dishes. He disappeared before Fig could even attempt to protest, leaving her alone with Mark, which she assumed was his actual plan all along.

"I'll wash, you dry?" Mark asked, and Fig nodded. She took her place beside him at the sink, towel in hand.

They wouldn't have had many dishes to wash if her dad weren't such a messy cook. Mark had a particularly hard time getting the grease out of the stir-fry pan, but at least it gave them a task to focus on. Fig didn't feel the need to talk, just clean. The one good thing about Mark being around was that usually this was her job, all on her own. Now they'd get it done quickly, and she could go back to her room and shut out the two of them.

She especially wanted to shut out Mark, who she was hesitant about from the start, and who she eventually allowed into the life and world she and her dad shared—into her dad's heart, apparently, too. She allowed him to bring her dad home from a storm. She went to him when her dad was spiraling. She trusted him to get them all home.

Or, wait, no. Her dad was the one who let Mark in. He was the one who let Mark understand him in ways that Fig never could, ways that she always tried to but failed at because he never opened himself up to her.

Mark was on the last dish when the first few notes rang out from the nook, and Fig nearly dropped the plate she was drying.

"Something wrong?" Mark asked.

Fig put the plate down and slowly shook her head. "No, it's just . . . He's playing my song," she told him. "That's my song."

Mark reached over to turn off the running faucet, even though he wasn't finished with the dish in his hands. They stood side by side, not moving, just listening, as her dad sat in another room playing notes Fig knew by heart.

"It's beautiful," Mark whispered.

Fig nodded, tugging at her earlobe as she blinked back tears.

Mark pulled her hand away from her ear. Maybe he already knew she couldn't control it, even when her ear hurt, just like he already knew her dad couldn't control his mind sometimes. She turned to look at him, and he was looking at her with soft eyes, his eyelashes gray like her dad's, his forehead creased. She wondered if he'd heard the song, from start to finish, that her dad wrote and named after him. And if he had, she wondered if he had any idea what the music meant. If he knew what it was like to love a man who could so easily get lost in his music and his mind. If he loved her dad. If he knew—and Fig now knew so clearly—that her dad loved him.

"It's his way of saying he loves me," she said.

Mark frowned. "He says that all the time, though."

"No. I mean, yes, he does. But this is different. This is more than with words. This is the part of him that he sometimes loses. This is how he lets me be a part of that. Because he wrote it, because he plays it." She shrugged. "That's what he told me, anyway."

Fig looked Mark right in the eyes, daring him to understand her.

He turned away, looking instead out toward the hallway where her dad's piano sat, pushed back in a corner of his nook.

"Just . . ." She paused. But then she squared her shoulders. "Just don't hurt him, okay?"

Mark kept his gaze focused down the hall, and the two of them listened to her song—to "Finola"—without moving or speaking, until the final notes played out around them.

# AT ETERNITY'S GATE

"YOU REMEMBER MY NEIGHBOR MARK?"

Fig didn't expect Danny to actually respond since he hadn't really engaged with her outside of shrugs and grunts lately, but she kept trying anyway. She missed him, missed discussing art with him and having someone to talk to about her dad.

She missed her friend, plain and simple. Maybe it would be like with the other kids at school, and if enough time passed, Danny would forget about the weirdness between them. Fig just hoped he wouldn't move on from her if he did.

As Fig anticipated, Danny just shrugged.

"Well, he's dating my dad."

For the first time in weeks, Danny fully faced her, his eyes wide. "He *what*?"

"My neighbor Mark is dating my dad."

They were standing by his locker, where Danny was getting his textbooks. He closed the locker door but didn't move, just continued gaping at her instead. "But they're both boys!"

Fig scowled. "What's wrong with that?"

Danny had the good sense to look chastised. "Nothing! I didn't mean . . . I didn't know your dad was gay. You never said."

"He's not," Fig started, but then stopped. "I mean, he wasn't before. Or . . . I don't know. He's never been with another guy before." She paused again. "But he's never really been with *anyone* before."

"Guess we don't need to worry about getting him to meet Miss Williams, then." Danny began walking down the hallway. Fig followed him. "This works, too, though," Danny added.

Fig stopped walking. "What do you mean 'this works'?"

Danny turned to look at her, his eyebrows pinched together. "Because it's the same thing we were going to try to do with Miss Williams. You said so yourself. Like Vincent and Theo."

"That's not what I said and it's *not* the same thing!" Fig said. "She . . . Mark and my dad . . ." She was finding it too hard to explain. "The point was to *understand* him, not change him!"

Danny was frowning at her, though she didn't know why. The warning bell rang. "I thought the point was to make your dad happy. I thought we were trying to help him."

"It was. We *are*."

"Then what's the problem?" Danny asked. The hallway around them was nearly empty as students filed into their classrooms. "What was the point of all those days in the library and all the books you got and the time I spent Googling?"

Fig blinked back sudden tears. "You don't understand. You can't."

Danny shook his head. "No, what I can't understand is *you*, Fig. I need to go to science. I'll see you around."

He left her standing in the middle of the vacant hallway, taking deep breaths to keep from crying. She felt so far away from Danny, so far away from her dad.

It was the confusion of it all—and maybe a smidge of desperation—that landed her at the library after school that day. She didn't have her dad, and she didn't have Danny. But she had Van Gogh and Hannah, and she sought solace in both of them.

"Oh, good, it's you," Hannah said as Fig approached the counter. The scent of vanilla, of Hannah, filled Fig's nose. "I've actually got something for you, hang on."

Fig's stomach did flip-flops as Hannah bent down behind the counter, unzipping her backpack that she stored back there. She pulled out some papers and handed them to Fig. "My brother is taking a psych class, and he had all these articles on mental illness. I thought you might want to check them out."

Heat spread up the back of Fig's neck as she reached for the papers, her fingers brushing against Hannah's as she did. Hannah had seen something and thought of her; Fig wanted to keep these articles forever. "Thanks," Fig mumbled as she placed the Van Gogh book she had tucked under her armpit on the counter. "Can I check this out, please?"

"Haven't you already read this, like, four times by this point?" Hannah asked.

It was the truth. Fig didn't even know why she was taking it out again; she didn't really want to reread it. She just liked that it was filled with the familiar letters Van Gogh wrote to his brother, filled with the familiar paintings that she knew by name and by heart and had spent months going to sleep thinking about—and she wanted to have it by her side.

"So, where've you been?" Hannah asked. "I feel like I haven't seen you or your boyfriend in forever."

Fig's eyes went wide. "Danny isn't my boyfriend."

"Oh. Sorry. You're just so cute together." Hannah waved it off and began to check out the book.

Fig put her hand down on it, stopping Hannah from her job. "We're not. He's just my friend."

Hannah held up her hands. "Sorry. I didn't mean to hit a nerve."

"You didn't, I just . . ." Fig took a deep breath. "I don't like boys like that."

Hannah's eyebrows shot up a bit, but she smoothed them back down and shrugged. "Oh. Cool. I get it."

*Did she?* Did she understand the things Fig felt, that Fig herself sometimes didn't know how to explain? The things she confided in her dad, even though her dad couldn't do the same? Fig wanted to know what her dad felt, if he liked the way Mark's face looked when they met, if Mark's smile made him feel warm like Hannah's smile warmed her. Fig wanted to know which one of them was brave, which one made the first move, took that first risk. Maybe they both took a risk together. Fig wanted to understand her dad's mind—always had, and never did—and the closest she came was this moment here, with Hannah, while he was home with Mark.

She couldn't understand her dad's art or his music, but this . . . this maybe she could.

"I don't like Danny," Fig said, "because I like you."

For a moment, Fig felt good. She felt like she finally grabbed on to something she had been reaching for.

That was, until Hannah's smile dropped, and Fig's good feeling was immediately replaced by regret. "Look, you're a sweet kid, but I'm, you know, in high school and—"

"Oh, God," Fig said, backing away from the counter. "No, no, it's fine. I should go. I have to go."

"Your book, let me—"

Fig grabbed the Van Gogh book off the counter, not even waiting to see if Hannah was finished checking it out. She left behind the articles Hannah had printed for her, hurrying out the library doors.

She felt hot and stupid the entire walk home, and she was near tears when she made it to her street and saw an unfamiliar car parked in the driveway. Her stomach dropped, and she started running.

Fig threw open the front door, dropping her back-pack on the floor. "Dad?" she called out, rushing into the living room, where she found her dad with Mark and a third man Fig had never seen before. She was breathing heavily, her sweater hanging off one shoulder as she looked at each of them in turn.

Her dad offered her a smile, but Fig didn't want it.

"How was school?" he said. "David here is from CP and P. Just another check-in. All is good. Why don't you go get your homework started?"

Fig looked over at Mark, whose fingers were fidgeting against his thighs the same way her dad's often did, and then she looked over at David. He had folders in his hands (was one their file?) and a plastic bag containing the drug test. "Did you tell him about the doctors?" Fig's words were quick and desperate, and she focused back on David. "He's bipolar, they think, he's taking medicine now."

"It's all okay, darling. Just go get your homework started."

Both Mark and David were so much taller than her dad, especially as he slouched between them, and Fig felt even smaller standing there. She reached forward, grabbed her dad's hand, and pulled at him, wanting to get him away from the other men, wanting to get him over to his piano nook. "Play something for him, Dad, show him," she said.

"Fig, stop," he said. He reached for her shoulder to stop her from tugging at him, but she bent away and kept pulling. "Stop."

"You need to play, Dad. You need to *show* him. He needs to know."

She let go of him and ran over to the piano nook. Mark's piece was still sitting on the music stand, front and center. She yanked it off, the paper rustling in her hands. "Sit down and *play*, Dad!"

Mark moved to put a hand on her dad's shoulder, and David took a step forward, too. "I know these visits can be stressful," David said.

"You don't know anything!" Fig shouted.

"That's enough," her dad said, but it wasn't a reprimand. His voice was too small.

Fig threw the sheet music, the pages of Mark's song scattering as they slowly fell to the ground, and she reached out to grab her dad's shirt to try to pull him again. "Please, Dad, show him how you can play. Just play, Dad, *please*. Show him you're okay! Show him! They don't understand, Dad, you have to play!"

He pulled Fig close and cupped her face with his hands. His eyes were wet, his face scrunched up as he held her. "Darling, please. I'm sorry, please go to your room."

"Why don't we all sit down," David was saying.

But Fig didn't want to sit down with him and with Mark and her dad. She pushed her dad off her, grabbed her backpack, and ran into her room. She slammed the door behind her and threw her backpack across the floor, where it skidded and landed under her bed. She could hear the voices from the living room, though she couldn't hear what they were saying. She wondered if she had made things worse.

She tried to take deep breaths but couldn't, and she got down on her knees to reach for her backpack. It was next to the hurricane book from the library that her dad had ruined and she had hidden under her bed. The book that Hannah had been teasing her about, the book that was overdue and broken. She picked it up and ripped out the pages that were stuck together, ink smudged and wet. The binding was falling off, and she ripped off the cover as well and threw it across the room.

Because that wasn't satisfying enough, she grabbed the Van Gogh book from her backpack and ripped its pages out, too. Ripped right through the center of his self-portrait, and *The Starry Night*, and *The Yellow House*, and all the rest of it that was supposed to bring her closer to her father but couldn't. Maybe nothing ever would.

Fig flung her body onto her bed and buried her face in her pillow, wishing, *begging* even, to disappear.

Fig's dad knocked on her bedroom door an hour later. She was still facedown on her bed, and sent a muffled "Leave me alone" his way.

He ignored her and walked in anyway. "Can we talk?"

Fig didn't know what to say. She wondered if this was how her dad sometimes felt, if she finally could relate to him. Everything was slowly slipping out of her grasp, and try as she might to hold on to normalcy, she couldn't get a strong-enough grip.

Her dad sat on the edge of her bed, and she curled into herself, facing the wall and away from him. "He's gone, love. He left."

"Mark?" she asked.

Her dad released a shaky exhale. "The man from CP and P."

"Mark's still here, then?"

Her dad reached out to tuck a strand of hair behind her ear. "Tell me what happened out there. What's going on in this beautiful head of yours?"

Fig didn't respond.

"We need to talk about this." His fingers were still running through her hair, moving the strands out of her face and behind her shoulder. "Me playing a bit of music isn't going to fix things."

Fig rolled over to look at him. "What will, then?"

"I'm taking care of it. You just need to worry about you."

She turned back to face the wall. "I want to be alone, Dad."

He didn't leave right away, just continued playing with her hair as she closed her eyes tightly and tried to forget.

She couldn't sleep that night, even after her dad surrendered and let her be. She couldn't get her mind to stop moving. She tugged on her earlobe so hard, it was sore by the morning. She stayed there, in her bed, not ready to leave it, using the fact that it was Saturday as her excuse to stay under the familiar comfort of her duvet. She rolled over to look at the clock. It was nine thirty, and Mark was coming over for breakfast.

The house didn't smell like bacon, though, which worried Fig because her dad should have been up and cooking. He rarely slept in. When he did . . .

*When he did . . .*

She kicked off her blankets and jumped out of bed, and she wished she was surprised that her dad wasn't in the kitchen, wasn't in the living room or his piano nook or the bathroom. She found him still in bed, a blanket pulled up nearly over his head, facing the wall, curled into himself and still asleep.

It had been a while since he had had a bad day. He was supposed to be getting better. He was supposed to *be* better.

"Dad," she said. "Dad, get up."

He moaned and mumbled things that didn't make sense into his pillow. Fig doubted they were even real words.

"Get *up*. *Now*, Dad!" Her voice was nasty, but she didn't care.

There was a knock at the front door. Fig chose to ignore it. They didn't need Mark. They *didn't*.

She reached for her dad's shirt—got fistfuls of what she realized was Mark's sweatshirt—and pulled. "Get up! Get up, get up, get up!"

Another round of knocking.

"Stop, please, just stop." At least her dad was saying real words now, even if he was covering his head and turning his shoulder to keep her away from him.

She heard the door swing open, heard Mark calling, "Anyone here?"

He appeared in the threshold of her dad's bedroom with a shiny silver key in his hand, looking at Fig and her dad with nothing but concern in his eyes.

Fig was furious. "He gave you a key?"

"For emergencies," Mark said. He took a step to move for the bed, for her dad, but Fig held her ground and put her arm out, forcing him to keep his distance.

"I know what I'm doing," she said. "He's fine. I've done this before."

"Let me help, Fig. I want to be here for him. For both of you."

"Fat lot of help you were yesterday!" Fig yelled. "I don't want you here. He's *my* dad. I'm the one who's done this before. I know how to take care of him, and I'm good at it, and I've always been good at it, and you don't know what you're doing."

Her dad groaned, pulled the pillow out from under his head to hold tightly in his hands instead.

"Fig, please," Mark said. *"Please."*

*"No."*

"Shut up!" Her dad's voice rang out, making her and Mark both jump. "Just shut up and get away from me!"

The pillow in his hands was launched at Fig's head, and it barely missed her as she ducked out of the way. Something snapped, then, all the anger that was building. She felt it move from her stomach to her fists as she climbed onto her dad's bed and started hitting him. "I'm trying to help!" she shouted at him. "I've always just wanted to help!"

"Fig, Fig, stop." Mark's hands wrapped around her waist, pulling her off her dad, even as she continued to swing her arms.

She felt her elbow connect with Mark's cheek, but he didn't loosen his grip, and she didn't relent. "Get up, Dad! I'll call CP and P and make them come back! I'll let them take you away, I'll tell them to find my mom. I swear it, Dad! Get *up*!"

Somehow Mark managed to pull her out of her dad's bedroom and into the living room, where he collapsed onto the couch with Fig still in his arms, falling on top of him. The TV was still on from the night before, the storm map on the Weather Channel lighting up the room until Mark reached for the remote and shut it off.

Fig continued to fight against him in the sudden stillness of the room, even as he held her tighter. "Let go of me. Just let me go."

"Not going to do that, Fig."

His arms were strong but gentle, and the fight left her as quickly as it came. She wrapped her small arms around his larger ones, and she cried. She cried because her dad was sick. She cried because she thought she knew what she was doing, but she *didn't* know what she was doing, and he never got better, and she never understood why. "I thought he was getting better," she cried into Mark's embrace. "He was doing good."

"He still is," Mark said. "The doctors say this stuff takes time to get right. Sometimes medications need to be changed. Sometimes he'll still have bad days anyway."

"I wouldn't know," Fig said. "He doesn't talk to me about that."

Mark sighed, deep and heavy, into her hair. "He doesn't want to burden you, Fig. He wants you to get to be the kid."

"I want to be his Theo," she said. "I *am* his Theo."

"I know you are."

She pulled back to look at him. "You don't! You don't know, you don't understand. Theo was—"

"Theo took care of Vincent. He sent him money. He listened to him. He believed in him," Mark said, and Fig was momentarily stunned to silence. "Vincent needed Theo and Theo needed Vincent. I get it, Fig. I do."

Her eyes searched Mark's. "How?"

"You're not the only one who can read." He shrugged. "You were so hung up on it all, and then we went to MoMA, and I just . . . I wanted to see why."

She was caught between wanting to yell at him to mind his own business, and wanting to cry because there was someone who noticed her enough to piece together her mind the way she was trying to do with her dad's.

"It's because of him." Mark didn't ask because he *knew*, and Fig felt understood for the first time in such a long while. "I see that. I get that."

"I didn't mean it," she said. "I don't want them to take him away, and I don't want to leave him. What if next time they come on a day when he's like this?"

"Then we explain to them that he's doing his best."

"What if that's not enough?" Fig asked. She reached over Mark for the remote control to turn the TV back on. She squinted at the sudden brightness from the Weather Channel, at the radar map that showed possible storms swirling and growing and waiting to happen. "What if there's another storm? What if he gets hurt?"

"I won't let him."

"You can't stop him. I can never stop him." Fig covered her face in her hands. "I want him better so that he can be my dad. I just want my dad. Why won't he tell me anything anymore? Why can't I understand?"

Mark moved her hands out of the way and wiped the tears off her cheeks in that gentle way her dad always did. His own eyes were bright and wet. "What do you want to know?" he said. "Ask me here, right now. We'll talk about this. I'll explain what I can to you."

Fig searched his face. "Really?"

"Really."

Fig's chest started to feel lighter as they began to talk. And it wasn't the first time she fell asleep with her head on Mark's lap, with his arm wrapped around her keeping her close and safe, but it was the first time that she did it without being scared, without her dad waking up alarmed and yelling. Instead, when her dad finally managed to stagger out of his bedroom, he collapsed on the couch with them.

The movement of the couch as he sat down stirred Fig from sleep, but she didn't mind, especially not when he lifted her legs to rest them on his lap and ran a hand through her hair. When Fig looked up at him, his eyes were closed again as he rested his cheek against Mark's shoulder.

# PART THREE

## November

*And I tell you,*
*the more I think it over,*
*the more I feel that there is*
*nothing more truly artistic*
*than to love people.*

—Vincent van Gogh to his brother Theo,
September 1888

# TWILIGHT, BEFORE THE STORM

FIG WOKE UP AND FLIPPED THE CALENDAR PAGE OVER. New month, clean slate. Thirty days until the scheduled follow-up meeting with CP&P. They were getting so close.

The new month, however, didn't bring many changes at school. Danny still wasn't really speaking to Fig. Try as she might, he wasn't budging, and Fig started not really speaking to Danny. She felt guilty that, after everything, Hannah turned her down (thinking about Hannah still made her stomach hurt, so she was avoiding the library). But even if Hannah hadn't existed, Fig didn't think she'd want to be more than best friends with Danny. She couldn't help that, couldn't control how she felt.

Danny understood that her dad couldn't help how his mind worked. Why couldn't he understand this?

Still, Fig missed him.

Especially when, in English class, Mrs. Lovotti paired them off to peer edit their sentences. Danny no longer sat close, and since Mrs. Lovotti had already paired Haley with Madison, she decided to pair Ava with Fig. Ava hadn't so much as looked at Fig since her Halloween party.

They switched papers without making eye contact and started to make edits on each other's work without comment. Fig corrected all of Ava's *its* to *it's* (and vice versa) while Ava rested her cheek in her hand, drawing doodles on Fig's page, even though Fig was pretty sure she had mixed up all her *lies* and *lays*.

"When you're done correcting your partner's papers, exchange back and explain what you did," Mrs. Lovotti said.

Which meant that Ava and Fig were going to have to talk to each other.

Fig tried to go first. "I think the first one needs to be *it's* with an apostrophe because you mean to say *it is*."

"I'm not mad at you," Ava said, and Fig's eyes snapped up to hers. Ava, finally, was looking right back at her.

"What?" Fig asked.

"I'm not mad. About the party. I thought maybe you thought I was."

"Oh," Fig replied, not knowing what else to say.

"Well, I mean, I guess I was? Because your dad kind of made it weird, you know? But then my mom talked to me about it." Ava shrugged, going back to her doodles. "She said that you and your dad have a lot going on right now."

Fig found herself nodding, hope and butterflies swirling in her stomach at the thought that someone was finally starting to understand.

"So, anyway. She told me to invite you over more. Like, for dinner, if you want, whenever. I'm just not allowed at your house."

Fig looked back down at their grammar sheets, at the corrections they both made. This was what she wanted, wasn't it? To be included. For Ava to realize her dad was sick and ask Fig to hang out anyway.

But it didn't feel right. Fig wasn't sure why she felt like crying.

"Okay, settle down now," Mrs. Lovotti interrupted from the front of the classroom. "Move your seats back, and let's go over the things you fixed."

Ava moved back to her seat, then leaned over to whisper to Haley, and Fig thought she would feel better. She thought that the idea of being invited over to Ava's house would start to make things feel normal again.

Haley laughed a little too loud, and Mrs. Lovotti yelled at her to hush. Ava didn't turn back around to look at Fig even once the rest of class.

Molly was sitting on the front steps when Fig got home. She had her phone on her lap and was looking up at the clouds. When she saw Fig approaching, she smiled. "Hi, Fig."

It made Fig nervous to see Molly outside and not inside with her dad. "Is my dad not answering the door? Did he cancel on you?"

"No! No," Molly was quick to say. "I had a half day today, so our lesson was early. I'm just waiting for my mom. She's running late."

"You can wait inside if you want."

Molly scrunched up her freckled nose, biting her lip with a smile. "I didn't want to be in the way. Your dad's boyfriend is over."

Fig's shoulders tensed, and she dropped her backpack to take a seat on the steps next to Molly. "He's not his . . ." Fig stopped. Because she supposed Mark *was* her dad's boyfriend. "They wouldn't have minded," she said instead.

"That's okay. I wanted to watch the sky anyway. We're supposed to get a big storm, I wanted to see if it was starting to come."

Fig had to put her hands on the step beside her to steady herself. She hadn't thought about hurricane season recently. The Weather Channel was on their TV much less these days. "What? What storm?"

Molly reached up to toy with the edges of her glasses. "I'm hoping they're wrong and it won't actually be so bad."

"What storm, Molly? When?"

"Tomorrow night," Molly said, turning to look at Fig, her forehead creased. "Are you afraid of storms? I *hate* them."

Fig's exhale was shaky. "I hate them, too." She *was* afraid of storms because of what they did to her dad, because he loved them and she couldn't understand that.

Molly did not love them. For a moment, Fig wanted to ask her to stay, to brave the storm with her, so Fig would not have to brave it alone. But then Molly's mom's car pulled up, and Molly stood, brushing off the back of her pants. "Maybe they'll be wrong," Molly said. "About the storm."

Fig slowly nodded. "Maybe."

Molly's mom barely had time to pull away before Fig burst through the front door. Mark and her dad were sitting on the living room couch, watching the weather broadcast on TV. Mark's eyes met hers across the room.

She had never felt more connected to Mark than in that moment, as they held each other's gaze before turning to face her dad. He looked delighted.

They didn't talk about the storm during dinner. Fig kept glancing out the kitchen window at the clear blue sky, as if it could change any second—which it could. The storm could blow in and cover the town and their home in darkness and pour rain down on all of them.

For now, Fig focused on the sun as it shone through that window as Mark told them in excruciating detail about the siding he put on a house that afternoon. She played her part in the conversation, recounting every boring second of what they learned about Mesopotamia in social studies. All the while, her dad asked questions in the appropriate places, but his eyes were unfocused. He barely ate his chicken.

Medication or no medication, her dad never could resist the pull of a good storm.

They left the dishes unwashed in the sink. No one had the patience for them, least of all her dad, who pushed his unfinished plate away to stand at the window instead of eating. "Love watching a storm roll in," he said, his face against the glass, fogging it up with his breath. "When did they say it'd be here?"

"Not until late tomorrow afternoon at the earliest," Mark said, then turned to Fig. "There's a chance it could go out to sea instead, though."

"Can we go for a walk?" Fig's dad asked.

"It's late, Tim. Just come sit with me."

"Just a short walk. Just to see the sky before the storm."

"Why?" Fig found herself asking. She wanted to say more, but when she opened her mouth, she could again ask only, "Why?"

"Because it's beautiful."

"No, it's not. It's *terrifying.*"

Her dad squinted at her, the sun from the window in his eyes. Fig stayed in her chair, gripping the sides of it so tightly her hands hurt. "It's all right, Fig," he said. "I've been taking my meds. I've been . . . I've been taking care of myself like the doctor said. I need you to find a little faith in me."

How could she put faith in something she couldn't comprehend? How could she be sure he wasn't going to be manic?

"It's just a walk," he said, then looked over at Mark, who had been quiet throughout the exchange. "And I swear on my mother's eternal soul that I'll stay home all day tomorrow."

Fig glanced at Mark, wondering if he believed that any more than she did.

But Mark sighed, and Fig was mad at him as he conceded. "Just a short walk," he said, and turned his attention back to Fig. "You want to come?"

She hesitated but shook her head. Her dad kissed her on the cheek as he went with Mark out the door.

On the school bus the next morning, the Ramirez siblings all had their fingers crossed that it would storm so bad they wouldn't have school the following day. The oldest Ramirez kid had a math test he wanted to get out of. The youngest one loved lightning.

Fig held her breath until their conversation changed to something else. She imagined the youngest Ramirez brother staring out the window in his bedroom, watching storm clouds roll in and counting the time between lightning strikes and the sounds of thunder, like her dad taught her to do. She remembered being younger, and her dad hoisting her up to watch through the window as lightning lit up the sky. "Now, start counting," he'd say, and she would.

*One Mississippi, two Mississippi . . .*

"It's getting closer," he'd say, cuddling her close, not realizing, even back then, she was wishing it would move farther away.

She couldn't focus in school. It was as if her mind were flipping between channels, focusing for a moment on the ones that showcased the weather and quickly passing ones that had to do with math or science or social studies. Nothing but white noise and emergency broadcasts.

This, she realized, was what her dad meant when he sat her down and told her about the buzzing in his head. She wished he could have told her how to get it all to slow down.

Maybe neither of them would ever know.

Fig's head got a little clearer in art class as she put the finishing touches on her painting. Her mind focused on one brushstroke at a time, following the lines of the thick black paint that completed the piece. She signed her name, small but clear along the bottom: a simple *Finola*. The same way that Van Gogh did with his *Vincent*.

"Oh, cool." Madison leaned over her desk. "Yours came out so good, Fig."

"Thanks," Fig said. She wanted to tell Madison the painting was about her dad, but she couldn't find the words. She looked over at Danny, who was nearly done with his own art. She wanted to tell him she loved his painting. She wanted him to look at hers and understand what it all meant. Neither of which happened.

She glanced back down at her painting, and for a moment, she wanted to rip it in half and forget about Van Gogh and her dad and everything.

"Okay, class, listen up," Miss Williams said. "You've had plenty of time all marking period, and you should be finishing these up this week if you haven't already. I need them dried and ready to go so that they can hang without making a mess in the auditorium, and I want to display everyone's work, so please try and get these done."

Miss Williams began moving from student to student, handing out a flyer. "This has all the information for your parents. It says what time you should be at the festival, and there's a form to fill out with a parent's signature. Make sure you return these to me by the middle of next week. There's a box to let us know how many people will be attending, and that's important for the PTA, so please don't forget."

When she got to Fig, Miss Williams didn't immediately hand over a form. "Fig, that's wonderful," she said as she looked at Fig's finished painting. "I know art has never been your favorite, but I'm proud of you."

"Do you understand it?" Fig asked, her fingers tugging her earlobe. "Do you think anyone will?"

"I think I do, but in art, when it comes to understanding, well . . . It's not always about what the art is *supposed* to mean. It's about what it makes people feel."

Fig thought about it. "What does my painting make you feel?"

Miss Williams smiled and handed Fig a flyer. "It makes me feel like calling my dad—even though we never really know what to say to one another—just to say hello. Just because I haven't in a while. Make sure you get this form to your dad, okay? Don't forget."

The bell rang, and as usual, everyone began gathering their things, putting away paints and tossing their used brushes in the sink. Everyone who had finished their paintings put them gently on the racks to dry. Fig was the last to finish, walking slowly so as to not let a single brushstroke drip as she put away her painting.

Danny was waiting for her at the door, which he hadn't done in weeks. He didn't smile at her, didn't look into her eyes, but at least he was waiting. "I wanted to say, well, be careful," he said. "With the storm. Because I know your dad gets weird about them."

Fig exhaled. "Thanks," she said.

They hovered at the door for a moment. Fig shifted her backpack to her other shoulder, and Danny bounced slightly on his heels. "Well, I should go to science."

"Okay," Fig said, and Danny turned to leave.

The sky was dark by the time Fig got off the bus. She zipped her coat as high as she could to protect herself against the harsh wind that came as a prelude to the storm. Georgina was a category 2 hurricane. Not the worst, but still, any storm that brought lightning and thunder also brought floods. Those storms knocked down trees and power lines. They reached that part of her dad that Fig never could.

It started to rain. Large, cold drops fell down Fig's nose and cheeks and made her shiver. The wind blew hard enough to whistle against the trees, and it was so loud she didn't hear the music until she was standing right there at the front door.

But once she heard it, she froze, her hand on the doorknob and rain falling in her eyes. Inside, her dad was sitting at the piano. He was safe from the storm, playing in that special way that made her feel like she was standing in a music hall with thousands of people in the audience, not in their small two-person home. The music was confident, and beautiful, and undeniably her dad's.

And it was Mark's song. The one her dad wrote and named for the man who somehow made her dad fall in love with him. Fig noticed that the windows of their home, as well as the ones in the yellow house across the street, were boarded up. With the same wood, even. In the same way. And she knew that Mark was there. Mark was inside, probably listening to her dad, who was sitting at his piano and not wandering outside, lost and staring at the sea. She never—*she could never*—get him to be anywhere but lost during a storm. She couldn't, not in years, get him to finish a piece, to sit and play it from start to finish, to stay in his head long enough to be with her and the music and not out in a storm.

Mark could. The rain was falling harder now; Fig was wet and cold. Still, she couldn't make herself open the front door. She couldn't make herself seek shelter. She didn't want to go inside, to see her dad at the piano, keeping his promise, with Mark comfortable in their home.

Fig didn't remember making the decision, but she dropped her backpack at the front door. Instead of going inside, she turned around and started walking.

Fig often wondered what her dad saw in the ocean, how he could stare at it for hours as if it held the answers to the questions in his mind, particularly during a storm, particularly when the ocean was most dangerous and she was most worried. In her research last year about hurricanes and tropical storms and weather patterns, she learned everything about how a storm starts, how it builds, how it blows in and destroys. The one thing she hadn't learned was why her dad loved storms, what it was about them that stole his mind from her.

She tried now to see what he did. She stood on the boardwalk, staring out at that ocean, wind and rain whipping at her face. Her dad's West Ham scarf was wrapped around her neck and mouth, but it was hardly a barrier from the weather. Behind her, all the shops were closed for the season and boarded up to protect them from storms. Everyone else was safely indoors somewhere—like her dad and Mark—and Fig stood alone, doing the very thing her dad did that she hated, wondering if a policeman would show up and drag her home.

Dark, angry purples and grays swirled in the sky as the rain poured down and met the ocean, which churned in shades of dark blue. Fig watched the waves rolling and crashing against the sand. It was like staring at a living Van Gogh painting. Fig walked to the edge of the boardwalk, squinting, wanting to see the impasto in those waves, the brushstrokes in the clouds.

Fig pulled off her shoes, leaving them with her socks at the end of the boardwalk so she could feel the cold, damp sand between her toes as she made her way to the water. The water, colder still, shocked her when the waves first hit her feet and crashed up her legs. But still, she dug her toes in and anchored herself.

She listened to the sounds: the crash of the waves, the howl of the wind, the drumming of rain against the wood of the boardwalk. Thunder rolled in the distance, vibrating up and down the beach. The cacophony was overwhelming, and it wasn't musical, wasn't something that she could hear and feel—something that reminded her of her dad.

The wind beat at her eyes, which started to burn from the rain and salt water, so she closed them tight. Her mind filled in the pictures. Was her dad as worried for her as she often was for him? Was he trying to understand where her thoughts would take her as she so desperately did with his?

Was he afraid for her? Was he angry with her? Was he feeling all the things he always made her feel?

Fig pictured him, young and brilliant, standing in the middle of an apartment with a spectacular view of New York City, with a baby in his arms he didn't know what to do with. Did he have bad days then, in that apartment, when Fig was too small to take care of herself? Did he spend days in bed as she cried in her bassinet, needing clean diapers and milk, needing *him*?

Vincent couldn't have been Vincent without Theo, and Fig could not be Fig without her dad. And maybe that was where she had got it wrong all along. Maybe that was why she was here, standing in a storm. Because she felt like she was losing him, and she wasn't his Theo, but he was *hers*, and she needed him and didn't know what to do now that he didn't need her.

"The sadness will last forever," Vincent had said to Theo, moments before he died. Fig thought maybe she could understand him now.

*"Fig!"*

She started thinking about curried spinach, and braids, and *darlings*—of piano chords and museums and starry nights. She started thinking of her father's arms and Mark's arms, and the comfort they gave each other that she wished they'd give her instead. She thought about the gap between Danny's teeth that she hadn't seen in so long because he wouldn't give her a smile, and Miss Williams's kind eyes and Hannah's crooked grin, and how she loved all those things and how they hurt her anyway.

*"Fig!"*

Lightning lit up the sky as she thought of yellow houses, and earlobes, and art. Of cypress trees and fig trees. Of Vincent and her father, forgetting for a moment where one ended and the other began. *One Mississippi, two Mississippi* . . .

"Fig!"

Strong arms suddenly wrapped around her waist just as another wave came crashing down on top of her, ice-cold water hitting her in the face and making her lose her footing. She fell, shaking and shivering and cold, and she heard her father's voice next as he held on to her tightly, falling with her. "Darling. Please, darling."

They both hit the sand, and it was wet and hard and smacked against her chin, and for a moment, the water covered both of them and she couldn't breathe. She fought against the waves, against the water and her father's hands, but he held her tight, and raised her up, coughing and shouting as he lifted his own head from the water.

"Mark! Take her! Just get Fig!"

Another strong arm wrapped around her, pulling her from the crashing tide, lifting her up. She opened her eyes to see Mark also grab a fistful of her father's sweatshirt—that Michigan State sweatshirt stolen from Mark after the last big storm. Mark yanked them both away from the shoreline, shouting, "I've got *both* of you."

Once they were far enough away to be safe from the reach of the waves, Mark released them both, falling back into the sand, gasping for air. Her father gathered Fig tightly into his embrace, trembling against her (or maybe it was Fig who was shaking) as he murmured, "Fig. Fig, my darling, what have I done? Oh, God, Fig."

Fig pushed against him, kicked her feet against the hard, damp sand. "Let me go, let me go!" she cried, her teeth chattering around the words.

Her dad only held her tighter.

"We need to go," Mark was saying. "We need to get out of the storm."

*"No!"* Fig kept fighting, kept shivering, kept crying. "Just leave me alone!"

"Never," her dad said into her ear, tears falling from his eyes onto her cheeks and down her neck as he tucked her head under his chin. She was too numb to feel the tears or the rain or the wind, but she stopped pushing against him, stopped trying to make him let her go. She buried her face in his chest, trying to find his warmth, to feel that he was really there.

Fig closed her eyes and shut out the rest.

# 16

# FISHING BOATS AT SEA

When Fig awoke, her back was pressed against her bedroom wall, and she was face-to-face with her dad, who was asleep next to her. His eyes were closed, and his breath was warm against her face. Sunlight shone through her curtains.

The storm was over.

She reached out, closing the small gap between them to touch one of his gray eyebrows with her finger, tracing slowly down the bridge of his nose. By the time she finished her journey, his eyes were open, looking at her. He closed them and leaned forward to press his lips against her forehead. When he opened them again, she offered him a weak smile and a cracked, "Hi."

"Good morning." His voice was a soft whisper but still seemed unnaturally loud in the quiet bedroom.

Fig felt . . . *exhausted*. Her arms and legs were achy, like before a fever begins. She tucked herself into a ball, curled closer into her dad. He wrapped an arm around her and pulled her closer still.

"Oh, my girl," he whispered into her hair. "I want to yell at you so bad. I want to lock you in this room forever."

He framed her face with his hands, and gently pulled her head up so he could look her in the eyes. "Why, Fig?" He swallowed, took a deep breath, and continued. "Why did you go out into that storm?"

Fig wanted to look away from him but couldn't. His eyes were wide and wet and so focused on her. "I wanted to see what you see," she told him.

His face crumpled, and tears fell down his cheeks (hers, too) as he asked, "Did you?"

She shook her head. "I don't think so."

He sighed. It sounded like relief. "I'm going to get you help. Okay? But I need to know when you're feeling this way. I need to know when things like this happen in that brilliant little mind of yours."

"Danny wanted to set you up with Miss Williams," she found herself admitting. "He thought it would help."

"Help?"

"You. Danny and I were trying to figure out how to help you," she said. "But Danny's not really talking to me anymore, and I've been so mad at Miss Williams because she called CP and P. I hate watching you get drug tested, Dad, and there are twenty-eight days until they come back, and that's twenty-eight days something can go wrong."

Her dad sighed. "Fig . . ."

"The kids at school treat me funny now. And I don't know what to do because I know it's not your fault, but I've been so mad at you." Fig took a deep breath. "And Hannah at the library helped me find books on Van Gogh and bipolar disorder, and I read a lot, but some of it was too hard to understand, and that made me angry because I wanted you to explain it to me, but you never did."

"Darling, I—"

"And I told Hannah I liked her, and it was stupid—*I* was stupid, because she's in high school and why would she like me?"

"She'd be a fool not to."

"I told you about her." Fig was crying now. "I told you about Hannah. Why didn't you tell me about Mark?"

"Oh, my girl. My darling." He pressed his forehead against hers. "I was *scared*."

"Of me?"

"Of loving Mark."

"Why?" Fig asked, her brow furrowed against her dad's. "Because he's a man?"

"No. Well, yes. But no." He shook his head with a soft laugh. "It's been so long. And I'm . . . You of all people know it's not easy loving me."

Fig shifted in the bed, letting her feet tangle in the blankets as she tried to move even closer to her dad. "Did you know that when Vincent van Gogh died, his brother Theo got sicker and sicker and—"

*"Fig."*

His voice was both sharp and broken, and she immediately stopped talking.

"I'm *not* Vincent van Gogh. I need you . . ." He took a deep breath. "I need you to stop seeing me as Van Gogh. I need you to see me as *me*."

She reached out to gently wipe the tears off his cheeks, letting her fingers follow the tracks they made down his face. Fig often saw her dad cry. That didn't mean it didn't hurt every single time. "I'm sorry," she finally said. "I'm sorry I went out into the storm."

"I'm sorry, too," he said. "And I'm going to get us both help, okay? We're going to figure this out. I love you, Fig."

"Double it."

"Love you, love you. Even more than that."

Fig pushed her face into his chest and let him hold her, let his fingers tap melodies against her back. "Was it my fault your mind got sick?"

She felt her dad still.

"What?"

"You were great before me. Your music was so great before me." Fig spoke into his shirt, mumbling against the fabric. "Everything was different . . . after me."

He pulled her away from his chest, cradling her face to look into her eyes. "Fig . . ." He paused, closed his eyes, and took a deep breath before continuing. "No. *No*. None of this is your fault. None of this happened because I had you. My life got so much better because I had you. And my mind . . . That just happened over time. Just because I'm sick. Just because it is. It was there before you, it got worse over time after you. But none of it was *because* of you. Do you understand that?"

Fig tried to be honest. "I don't know. I tried to read and learn. But I don't know that any of it makes sense."

He pulled her close again. "Then we will figure out how to make sense of it together." He pressed a kiss to her hair. "Is there anything else? Anything else you need to ask or tell me?"

She bit her lip. "Yeah."

"You can tell me anything."

She swallowed, thinking about the pouring rain and her drenched clothes. "My new phone was in my pocket last night."

There was silence. And then he was shaking, pressing his face into her hair as he laughed. His laughter was wet, and it was wobbly, but still it felt good to hear.

Fig was unsteady on her legs as they left her bedroom. Her dad insisted on making her some hot tea, and she didn't want to be alone, not yet, so she insisted on following him to the kitchen.

She stopped dead in her tracks when she saw Mark, asleep on the living room couch. Her dad turned to look back at her. There was a slight smile on his face. "He's probably exhausted."

Fig thought of her dad's bed, empty and not slept in right down the hall. "Why did he sleep on the couch?"

"Best guess is he wanted to guard the door from the both of us."

Fig quietly padded over to the rather small couch, which made Mark look like a giant. He was lying on his back with one foot placed firmly on the floor, as if he were ready in case he needed to get up quickly, as if he hadn't expected to actually fall asleep. She studied his face. Sometimes she forgot he was older than her dad, but other times she thought he looked just as haunted and worn. She wondered if loving and losing his wife and now openly loving her dad meant he was a lot braver than she was willing to give him credit for.

She reached her hand out, wanting to trace the curve of his nose like she traced her dad's, but she stopped, her fingers hovering in the air. She didn't know if she was allowed, if she had earned that right.

Fig lowered her hand, and Mark slowly blinked open his eyes, looking at her with both exhaustion and worry. "How're you feeling, sweetheart?" he asked, his voice rough and raspy.

Fig's throat felt tight. She couldn't answer him, so she nodded instead.

His eyes were so . . . so clear and blue and green, swirls of colors like a Van Gogh sky, and he smiled at her—a small smile but a real one. And those swirls of colors in his eyes grew blurry and wet (but maybe that was because her own eyes were filling with tears), and she knew, she just *knew*, that he would not leave them. He would weather the storm with them both.

She threw her arms around him and held him tight, and he held her right back.

# SELF-PORTRAIT AS A PAINTER

FIG'S DAD ASKED HER (AND ASKED HER AND ASKED her) if she wanted to stay home from school the next day. So she did. She, her dad, and Mark sat down and made plans (and made plans to make more plans). Mostly about things they would do together, appointments they would make, doctors they would talk to. Her dad even asked, hovering and worried, if she wanted to stay home the day after, too, but Fig couldn't stay home with them forever. She still had some things she needed to do alone.

When she went back to school, Fig found Danny before homeroom. She was slightly out of breath from pushing through the maze of students in their coats and carrying their backpacks and sports equipment as they climbed out of buses and their parents' cars.

"Hey," Fig said.

"Hey," he replied. "How was the storm? Was your dad okay?"

Fig figured a lie by omission was appropriate in this case. "He's okay."

"Oh, good."

Their homerooms were in opposite directions, but she followed him down the hall. "Danny, can I ask you something?" Fig said, stopping. If she didn't turn around now, she'd never make it to class on time.

Danny pulled on one of the straps of his backpack so it sat more firmly against his back. "What?"

She took a deep breath, pushing past the nerves in her stomach. "Did you only want to help my dad because you wanted to be my boyfriend?"

"What? No," he said, his eyes wide.

"I just don't understand why you wanted to help if you don't want to be my friend."

"I *did* want to be your friend," Danny said. "I picked up the paintbrushes your dad knocked over in class that day. I wanted to help him."

"But why?"

"Because my dad's sick, too," Danny said, and Fig gaped at him. "Well, not like your dad, not really. He's in rehab. I don't get to see him. This is his second time, but he can't help it, either. Just like your dad. My mom says there's nothing we can do, but . . ." Danny shrugged.

The warning bell rang.

"I should go," Danny said, and then turned to walk into his homeroom.

"Wait!" she called after him. And she worked up the nerve to tell him the one thing she wanted to all along: "I like Hannah."

Danny froze. "What?"

"At the library. I like her. Well, I did, anyway, but that's another story." She shook her head. "What I mean is, that's why I can't be your girlfriend. Because I liked Hannah, and you're my best friend."

"Oh."

"Is that okay?"

Danny just shrugged, looking down at his shoes.

Fig's stomach sank. "I'll see you in art class?"

"Yeah," Danny said. "I'll see you in art class."

After school Fig once again ran into her father's student Molly as she was leaving the house, her mom parked and waiting patiently in the driveway. Fig was surprised to see Molly. She didn't think her dad was giving lessons that afternoon. Fig and her dad had decided they needed to take time to sort things out, to go to their doctors and to take care of themselves. "Did you have a lesson?" Fig asked.

"Oh, hi!" Molly said. "No, I had to drop off a check. And, well, I was hoping to maybe bump into you."

"Me?"

"Yeah," Molly said, and then hovered on the front stoop. Fig was about to say that she should go before her mom honked the horn, but Molly, in one quick breath, said, "Maybe you want to hang out sometime?"

Fig blinked. "Really?"

"If you want to. I could give you my number. Or, I guess your dad has it. But maybe I can come over sometime without having a lesson," Molly said, her eyes open wide, and Fig really looked at them for the first time. They were brown with bits of gold, like sunflowers, and they matched the color of her hair when the sun hit it just right. "I really like you, Fig."

*"Me?"* Fig said again.

Molly laughed as her mom honked the car horn.

"She's getting impatient," Molly said. "So, do you? Want to hang, I mean."

Fig hesitated. "Sometimes . . ." She took a deep breath, looking down at her feet. "Sometimes my dad doesn't feel well. He's . . . sometimes he's . . ."

"I know," Molly said, and Fig's eyes snapped up to look into hers. "My mom told me that's why he cancels lessons sometimes. But maybe when he has a bad day, you can come to my house if you want."

Fig didn't know what to say to that. "Oh."

"So . . . ?" Molly asked as her mom honked again.

"Yes!" Fig exclaimed a little breathlessly. "Yes."

Molly smiled. Fig really liked that smile.

When Fig walked inside, her father was waiting on the other side of the front door. "Just got off the phone with your teacher, Miss Williams."

Fig dropped her backpack. "School literally just got out."

"I appreciate her being on top of things. She thought it was important."

"Well, was it?" Fig asked, and glanced about the house. "Where's Mark?"

"Working. Some people do that."

"You finished a song," Fig pointed out. "That's work."

"Not work until I sell them."

"So sell them."

"You make it sound so easy."

They were already off track. "What'd Miss Williams want?"

He shook his head, as if he were unclogging his ears after jumping into a pool. He had explained to Fig that sometimes his medications made him foggy, and he had asked her to be patient with him—and never to let him off the hook. "She said you brought some flyer home you were supposed to give me. She wanted to make sure you did, and if you didn't—which you didn't—to make sure I knew to come to this Fall Festival. Apparently my daughter has quite the painting to show off."

Fig felt herself blushing.

"Why didn't you give me this flyer? Go get it."

Fig didn't move.

"What's wrong?" She went to tug on her earlobe, but he reached out and gently pulled her hand away. "We said we're going to be honest with each other, yeah? Even when it's hard? You've mentioned this festival before. I know you're excited about it. So why not give me the flyer?"

"It was . . . a long couple of weeks."

"Understatement of the century, darling, but that doesn't really answer my question."

"It's too soon. You've got that doctor's appointment, and the CP and P visit is . . ." She glanced over at the calendar, where so much of November was already crossed off. "Five days later." She shrugged. "It's not the right time, that's all. And they'll let me bring the painting home when it's over, so you'll get to see it anyway, and—"

"The flyer, Fig."

Fig sighed and unzipped her backpack. She pulled out a folder and found the flyer for the Fall Festival right in the front, with black paint smudges on the corner from where she grabbed it after finishing her work. She pulled it out, handed it to him, and watched as he read the information carefully, holding the flyer close to his face as he scanned it.

She wondered if he realized the school's enrollment was at an all-time high, and that—between the teachers and everyone's families—the auditorium that looked so big when empty was going to be full and loud and feel much smaller. That there would be science experiments, and art, and readings. That the Fall Festival would be an event overrun by middle schoolers, and the commotion would be . . . a lot. And that was if he had a good day at the doctor's. That was if he had a good day at all.

"It's okay if you can't go, Dad." She meant every word, and she wanted him to know that.

Her dad's eyes didn't leave the flyer. "If it's okay with you, I'd still like to try."

Fig nodded, didn't know what else to say. "Okay."

On the day of the festival, the students had to be at the school to set up before it started, and Fig's dad and Mark were at his doctor's appointment. They were talking about insurance and medications, options for therapy for Fig, and several other things they told Fig not to worry about.

So Fig stood alone in front of her painting, while parents and teachers and other family members began filling the auditorium. She and Danny stood side by side, not really talking, in that crowded auditorium in front of paintings they were both proud of. But Fig found she was nervous for anyone to look at hers.

"I don't care that you like girls," Danny suddenly said. Fig almost didn't realize he was speaking to her.

"What?"

Danny shrugged. "It just sucks that you like Hannah and not me."

"I can't help it, Danny."

"I know," he said, looking down at his feet. "It just sucks, okay?"

Fig nodded. It hurt when Hannah didn't like her back, which was why she now avoided the library. "It sucks not having you for a friend."

Danny exhaled deeply, and then he gave her a shy smile that made her breathe easier around him for the first time in weeks. "Yeah," he said.

Danny's art club teacher from the library suddenly interrupted them, wanting to see his work. He gave Fig one last glance and a little wave, and she felt even more alone as he turned away from her to show off his painting.

Fig glanced at the clock—it had been only about a half hour since parents were allowed to come in. There was still time for her dad to show, but the possibility was feeling more and more unlikely. She kind of wanted to go home.

"Hey, you," Miss Williams said, making Fig jump. "Oh, didn't mean to scare you."

"Hi," Fig said.

"Some of your other teachers asked me about your painting. They were impressed."

Fig didn't respond.

"You know, your dad and I chatted for a bit the other day on the phone. I wanted to touch base with him after everything you and I spoke about. He . . . he likes to talk." Miss Williams laughed as Fig rolled her eyes. "Oh, it's sweet, though. He could talk about you for hours if I had the time, I'm sure. He told me a bit about what's going on at home."

Fig's cheeks grew warm. "Oh."

"He's very proud of you, Fig. And he told me he was going to do everything he could to try and be here tonight."

Fig frowned and once again looked at the clock. She nodded, unable to respond to Miss Williams, to tell her that she knew her dad loved her, she knew he would try, but she also knew that sometimes he just couldn't. And that was okay—really, it was—but still . . . It sometimes made Fig want to cry anyway.

"They come back in five days," Fig found herself saying. "Hurricane season ends then, too. I mean, there shouldn't be another storm. But there could be, for five more days, and that's when they come back."

Miss Williams blinked at her. "Who, Fig?"

"CP and P. Someone came after you called them, in September. And they came back, without warning, a bunch of times, so that they could make a report on my dad. In five days, they tell us what happens next. They'll tell us what they saw, what they think of my dad." Fig took a deep breath and looked back at her painting. "I don't know why I thought this would help."

Miss Williams sighed. “Fig . . .”

“Fig!” Ava’s voice suddenly rang out, interrupting them as she appeared with Madison and Haley. “A bunch of us are having our parents drive us over to the junction for ice cream. My mom told me to invite you. Do you want to come? She said she’d drive.”

Fig hesitated, and she felt Miss Williams’s eyes on her and all her old friends. She wanted to tug at her earlobe. She folded her hands together instead.

Ava’s mom told her to invite Fig for ice cream. Just like she told Ava to invite her to her house. No one had to tell Molly to ask Fig to come over. No one had to tell Danny to help in the first place.

Fig didn’t think Ava or Haley or Madison would ever really understand. She didn’t think she would ever be able to just hang out with them like they used to, pretending everything was okay. “Thanks, but I’m gonna wait here,” Fig said. “For my dad.”

Ava shrugged, and that was that. As the girls started to walk away, Fig had to force herself not to call them back, not to tell them she had changed her mind and wanted to go with them.

“Hey.” Miss Williams wrapped an arm around Fig’s shoulders. “In five days, social services will come to your house, and they will know that your dad loves you. And they will do what they can to help so that he can always be there to love you."

"He's not going to come today." Fig's nose burned. "And if he does, what if he's . . . not him? What if everyone laughs at him again?"

"Your dad has been doing everything he can so that doesn't happen. And there's still over an hour left," Miss Williams said. "Tell you what, if your dad can't make it, we'll call him, and I'll take you to get some ice cream to celebrate, okay? And you can even take the painting home right away tonight to show him."

"Or you and I can get ice cream together?"

Fig turned to find Danny beside her again, listening as he stood next to his *Sunny Day* painting, with his hands buried deep in his pockets.

"Really?" she asked.

"Yeah," Danny said. "Like you said, it sucks not being your friend."

Fig smiled her first real smile all day. But then she looked at the clock and sighed. "Thanks. Both of you. But I really don't think my dad's going to make it."

"Ye of little faith!"

Fig knew that voice, with its slight accent, knew that belligerent snark that only her dad could inject so much love into. She whipped her head around and saw her father standing there, right there at her festival, in the auditorium, with a smile on his face and Mark by his side. He looked a little pale, a little sweaty, but he wasn't sick, he wasn't making a scene, he was just there, *really there*—and she didn't even care if anyone was looking, didn't check to see if anyone was laughing, just ran the few steps it took to jump into his arms. It was a good thing Mark was there to brace him from the impact.

"You're okay," Fig said. "You're here."

"I had to endure Van Gogh for months. Had to come see this painting I've heard so much about."

He put Fig back onto her feet, and she finally got to introduce him to her best friend. "Dad, this is Danny—Danny, this is my dad."

Her dad held out his hand toward Danny. "I hear you've been trying to help sort out my brain. I wanted to thank you properly for that."

Danny shook her dad's hand. "I don't think I actually helped much."

"I hear you helped plenty," her dad said. Danny blushed.

"Wow, you painted that?" Mark interrupted to ask, and Fig remembered why they were all there.

She grabbed her dad's hand and pulled him so that he was standing right in front of her painting. "It's supposed to be us, Dad," she told him, and then waited.

He was there, with her, but she still very much needed him to understand.

She couldn't find the nerve to look at him, but she heard him take a deep breath. His hand was slightly trembling in hers, but the rest of him grew still. "Yeah," he finally said, exhaling, and Fig found herself exhaling, too. "Yeah, Fig. That's us."

It was a piano. A black grand piano like the ones she saw him playing in photographs, like the one she knew he used to have in that apartment where she spent the first year of her life, with the view of New York City. The piano was him, everything that made him tick, with its black keys and white keys that made music that could so easily, without care, go out of tune. If Fig listened hard enough, she could almost hear one of her dad's songs coming from the piano. And out of the top, growing tall from the center, was a tree.

A fig tree.

Thanksgiving came. Fig's dad overcooked the turkey, and he and Mark argued when her dad left a burner on and accidentally scorched his apron.

Mark balled up the singed apron and threw it into the sink.

"I didn't mean to," Fig's dad said.

"You never *mean* to, Tim," Mark barked back. Her dad cringed, and Fig tried to keep her eyes on the potatoes she was overstirring. Mark wiped a hand across his face. "I'm sorry. I just . . . I didn't mean—"

"Yeah, you did," Fig's dad said with a shrug.

"Every day I wake up hoping I don't walk into chaos," Mark admitted. "Sometimes it scares me a little."

Fig's dad glanced at Fig before turning back to Mark. "You and Fig probably feel the same about that. I hate that I make you both feel that way."

Mark nodded and wrapped an arm around Fig's dad. "Come on," he said. "Let's finish this meal."

When dinner was ready, and they sat down at their small, three-chair table, Fig noticed that Mark's eyes were shining as he stared at the small turkey in front of them. "This is my first time actually having a real Thanksgiving dinner since Kate died," he confided.

"The cranberry sauce is from a can," her dad said, the familiar blush crawling up his neck to his ears. "The green beans were frozen, and I'd bet good money the turkey is dry. I'm English. I'm no good at this."

Mark laughed, scooting his chair closer to Fig's dad as he wiped at his eyes. "That doesn't matter, Tim. That's not the point."

They smiled at each other. And then they kissed.

Fig looked away, down at the food covering the table. Truth was, most years her dad picked up a rotisserie chicken. They watched the Macy's parade together, but it was just the two of them, so they didn't go through all the trouble of a big meal. This year, he tried. Maybe the turkey was dry and maybe the mashed potatoes were defrosted in the microwave, but he tried. For Mark, for her.

When Fig looked back up, Mark's eyes were on hers. Lately Fig wondered if her dad was right, and she and Mark had more in common than she was willing to concede. They both loved a man who sometimes hurt them. Not because he wanted to but because his mind sometimes failed him, and he needed help that wasn't always a perfect fix. They both wanted him to be okay.

What had Mark done in the years between his wife's death and this Thanksgiving? Did he go out to eat? Did he sit alone at his table?

"Do you want to carve the turkey?" Fig asked him.

"Me?" Mark said.

"We all know I'll make a mess of it," Fig's dad added.

Mark laughed. "Okay, okay." He took the carving knife from Fig's dad and leaned over the table. He brought the knife gently to the turkey, as carefully as he had brought the razor to her dad's face months ago.

With an artist's precision, he made the first cut.

Four days later, the woman from CP&P knocked on the front door. "Good afternoon, Finola. It's good to see you again," she said. Fig didn't even remember her name.

All the November dates were crossed off the calendar, up to the last square, with the number *30*, where *CP&P* was written and circled in the center. That morning, Fig was the one obsessively watching the Weather Channel for the extended forecast. It was the very last day of hurricane season. A cold front was coming, but the skies were blue. There was no forecast of rain at all that week.

Two big storms in one year had been more than enough. The sporadic CP&P visits throughout those three months had been more than enough. Fig didn't know what would happen when the lady left; she didn't know what would happen by the end of the day or the next morning, when she'd cross off the last day of November, and December would begin.

But it was time to find out.

The woman, who reintroduced herself as Linda, sat next to Fig on the couch. Fig tugged at her earlobe, and her dad pulled her hand away, holding it in both of his own.

"So, we've compiled a report the past few months, and I have to say, you should be proud of yourself, Mr. Arnold. It seems like you've worked very hard."

"I have," her dad said. "Fig's too important not to."

Linda smiled at Fig. "I've heard these past few months have been stressful for you," she said. "Do you want to tell me about that?"

Fig looked over at her dad, who nodded. She also looked over at Mark. "I was scared," she said. "Of losing my dad. But also . . ." Fig stopped short.

"Also *what*?" Linda prompted.

Fig tugged her ear. She couldn't help it. "I want him better. I don't want it to be like it was anymore. It's too hard, and I hate it." She turned again to her dad, her eyes blurry. "I'm sorry, Dad. I'm so sorry. Is that okay?"

Her dad sat on the other side of her, bringing his hand to her cheek before pushing a loose strand of hair behind her ear, one that had slipped out of the braid he did for her that morning. "Of course that's okay, darling. That's . . . God, that's why we're here. That's why your teacher called in the first place. It was too much, and you didn't deserve that. I know you've hated all of this, and *I'm* sorry. And I'm going to keep working to get better for you."

Fig took a deep breath, but her tears fell anyway. Her dad wiped them away.

"What happens now?" Fig asked.

Linda smiled. "That's what I'm here to discuss."

Fig sat on the softest couch she had ever sat on, surrounded by equally soft throw pillows that matched the lamp on the desk of the woman who patiently sat across from her, waiting for Fig to speak.

It was her first appointment, and her dad was having a bad day, so Mark had driven her. He was waiting right outside the door in case Fig needed anything.

She supposed she could talk about that, about her dad's bad day and about how Mark filled the broken bits of them like glue, like he fixed houses and helped fix her dad. She could talk about how Danny was her best friend even though he still liked her as more than a friend, and how she was nervous (and excited) to go over to Molly's house for the first time in two days. She could talk about how she was starting to blush around Molly the same way Danny sometimes still blushed around her, and how she hadn't yet gone back to the library because of her feelings for Hannah.

She could talk about how she'd counted down to November 30 because she thought that day would be the end, only to realize it was just the beginning. CP&P would still check in; her dad still had work to do. But

Fig knew that he was trying—trying new medicine, new doctors, new relationships—and Fig wanted to try, too.

So she and her dad would talk, and they would listen. To each other, to Mark. And for Fig, to her new therapist, who was patiently waiting for her to make the first move.

But Fig didn't know how.

Instead, she glanced about the room at the therapist's diplomas, surrounded by paintings, on the walls. Fig looked at the artwork but didn't recognize any of it. She liked the beachy paintings, though, images of the ocean crashing on the shore, of umbrellas stuck in sand and towels laid out to sunbathe on. "Do you know who painted those?" Fig asked.

Her therapist smiled. "I have no idea, actually, but I can find out. Do you like art, Finola?"

Fig nodded.

"Why don't you tell me about the kind of art you like?"

Fig smiled. She didn't know how she and her dad and Mark would always deal with CP&P check-ins, or her dad's bad days, or the next hurricane season. She didn't know how she could make sure her dad kept making music, didn't know how she could make sure Mark wouldn't leave. She didn't know how she could get the three of them to a point that meant they wouldn't have to worry about any of it.

But this? This she *could* do.

"What do you know about Vincent van Gogh?"

# September, Again

*The heart of man is very much like the sea,*
*it has its storms, it has its tides*
*and in its depths it has its pearls too.*

—Vincent van Gogh to his brother Theo,
November 1876

# FINOLA

"YOU GOTTA STAY STILL."

"I can't. I can't."

"You can. Just try and breathe."

Mark was tying her father's tie. Or at least attempting to. Her father was sweaty and practically vibrating, shifting his weight from one foot to the other, fidgeting with the cuffs and buttons of his dress shirt. He was nervous. He was making Fig nervous, too.

The weather reporter on the TV was talking about Hurricane Reese making its way to the coast, expected to hit landfall on Long Island sometime in the next few days.

But today was all sunshine, feeling like summer, with the scent of salt water from the ocean in the air. Fig turned off the TV. No one was paying any attention to it anyway.

What a difference a year made.

"Tim, I can't do this if you don't stay still," Mark said.

Her dad had a clean-shaven face and neatly trimmed hair. His black trousers were pressed, his shirt crisp and ironed. His jacket hung over one of the kitchen chairs. His hands were jittery—they played familiar notes in the air, on Mark's arms—but they weren't trembling. He looked good. He was ready. Fig and Mark just had to get him there.

Fig was still in her pajama pants and a tank top, and Mark in a sweatshirt and gym shorts. They would get ready together later. For now, everything was about her dad.

She watched as Mark finally got her father to stay still long enough for him to finish tying his tie and to smooth out the collar of his shirt with a gentleness that seemed to calm her dad. "You look nice in a suit," Mark said, breaking into the smile he reserved for the two of them.

Her father couldn't help himself, and he raised his eyebrows with an, "Aye, aye?"

Mark laughed. “Everyone in that room tonight is going to see what I’ve always seen.”

Her father’s grin grew sheepish. “And if I mess it all up?”

“I’ll still see it anyway,” Mark said.

That made Fig smile.

Her dad was writing music again. Not every day, not always very good. But he was writing music and had sold a new piece, and now someone wanted him to perform. It wasn’t a huge music hall in London or New York City, but the Count Basie Theatre in Red Bank, New Jersey, was still a grand theater, with more than a thousand seats—enough to set her father on edge.

It set Fig on edge, too. The moments throughout the week when her dad sat with her and Mark on the couch watching TV before bed, with his fingers practicing their well-trained dances on her or Mark’s legs or arms or shoulders—or the moments when he sat unmoving at his piano bench, staring at the sheet music . . . Well, they worried her.

“Are you sure you don’t want me to drive you over?” Mark asked.

“No. No, I’m good. You two get yourselves ready and just . . . just be front and center once they turn those bloody lights on me, yeah?” He glanced around the room. “Where’s my Fig?”

She pushed off the wall she had been leaning against while watching the two of them. She had his jacket in her arms. “I’m right here.”

He smiled, and she held up the jacket for him. Once he had pulled it on, she brushed the back of it smooth, and then she wrapped her arms around him in a big hug that would probably leave wrinkles. She hoped he wouldn’t care, because she sure didn’t.

Fig didn’t tell him he’d be great, and he didn’t ask her to say that he would be. Instead, she confessed to him a long-kept secret: “I’ve always wanted to see you play like this.”

“Well then,” he said, with a slightly wonky smile, “in that case, I better make this the best gig of my life.”

Mark was quiet on the ride to the theater. “You’re nervous,” Fig said.

“I know he can do this,” Mark said, his hands gripping the steering wheel of his truck more tightly. “I just want him to know he can, too.”

Fig, in her new dress and shoes, stayed close to Mark as they navigated the crowd waiting to see her father. Mark offered her his arm, and she laced hers through it. She glanced at everyone standing around the waiting area and wondered if anyone had seen her father play in his past—in that different part of his life that sometimes seemed to belong to someone else. Mark looked as lost as she felt as they found a spot along a wall to wait for the ushers to let them go in.

Fig spotted Molly, standing in the center of the crowd with her parents, wearing a dress that matched her pale blue glasses. When Molly saw Fig, she made her way across the room, squeezing through the maze of the crowd to join her. "Hey! You look really pretty," she said.

Fig's cheeks were warm, and when she looked over at Mark, he was fighting back a smile. "Thanks, Molly," she said. "You look really pretty, too."

"I'm *so* excited to hear your dad play," Molly said.

The ushers were now taking tickets, and people started moving into the hall to take their seats. Molly's parents called Molly back over, and Mark started moving, too, but Fig froze. Mark looked at her, confused. "I'm nervous," she whispered. And then she quickly explained, "Excited. But nervous."

Mark nodded. He understood. "We promised we'd be front and center the moment they turn those lights on him," he said. "What do you say we go and keep that promise?"

The ceiling of the theater was high and arched, ornate with gold-painted patterns and chandeliers. The seats were clothed in red velvet. Fig gazed ahead to the stage, wide and high in front of them.

When the floor lights went down, Fig held her breath—and Mark's hand.

The stage lights illuminated a black grand piano. And front and center, sitting tall as if he belonged there—and Fig believed he *always* belonged at a piano—as if there were nowhere else in the world he could possibly want to be, was her father.

He looked taller, even seated there on a piano bench, than she'd ever seen him before.

Fig's father looked out into the crowd, and for a moment she saw that familiar expression in his eyes, the one that seemed to signal he was temporarily lost to himself. Fig had to fight the urge to run onstage and into his arms to shield him from what could prove to be an unforgiving audience.

But then, even across the bright lights and the large crowd, his eyes found hers. And that lost look disappeared from his face.

"This song is the most important piece I've ever written, and I'll never write anything that means more to me than this," he said.

He looked right at Fig and smiled.

"It's called 'Finola.' "

# ACKNOWLEDGMENTS

YOU HEAR A LOT ABOUT HOW STRESSFUL AND DIFFICULT the publishing journey is when you're trying to achieve it, but no one prepared me for how anxiety-inducing writing these acknowledgments would be. So many people have supported and helped me throughout the years, and the thought of leaving anyone out makes me want to curl up with Netflix and procrastinate.

(Which I did indeed do for a couple of days.)

But, because all of these people deserve their due, I'm going to suck it up and do my best to show how much I appreciate them.

I still remember having to change my clothes after sweating through them during my first phone conversation with my wonderful editor, Elise Howard, because I was so nervous. But she understood everything I set out to accomplish with this little story and promised me right from the beginning that Algonquin would take good care of Fig. Editor Krestyna Lypen has also been such a blessing, not only with Fig, but with dealing with my anxiety-ridden emails. And there are a lot of them.

To my entire Algonquin team, you have all kept that promise to take care of Fig and have done so with more heart and attention than I could have ever asked for. Thank you.

I also will never forget being at the gas station when my agent, Jim McCarthy, called me up to tell me that we had an offer. He laughed joyfully right along with me, as I was so flustered by the entire ordeal I popped my trunk instead of my gas tank. I couldn't ask for anyone better to trust my career and stories with—especially someone who knows exactly what I mean when I reference the *Bring It On* musical.

By now my parents are wondering when I'm going to mention them, so here you go, Mom and Dad. Thank you for buying me countless composition notebooks to fill with stories back when I was eight, and for allowing me to find my own path, even if we didn't know if that path would ever pay. I never felt like I couldn't go after my dream, and I never felt like that dream was impossible with your support in my corner. (And to my brother, Matthew, who didn't really do much to help my writing but has been a pretty solid brother, so I'll mention you anyway.)

I might have convinced myself it was all impossible, however, if not for my mentors, Donna Freitas and Eliot Schrefer. From you both, I've learned to be confident in both my writing and with who I am (even if Eliot makes fun of my inability to remember *passed* vs. *past*, and Donna will never let me live down the witch book I started at the beginning of my MFA program).

To Liz Welch, you are my Theo; I am pretty useless without you.

And to my wonderful group of friends who are willing to read draft, after draft, after draft (and who put up with my neurotic self while doing it): Christine Headley, Sarah Warren, and Briana McDonald—thank you for all those times I needed reminding that this was worth it. Viva la Fig!

As my debut novel, this is a coda of everyone who has helped me throughout the years, and while it will be impossible to name everyone, I need to try: my big Italian family (all of you Moseras and Sciallos), Laura DeVincenzo (for blessing me with fried Oreos, vinegar fries, and a godson), and everyone at Fairleigh Dickinson's creative writing MFA program, especially my MFA buddies, Ryan Whitaker, Mariella Diaz, and Ken Pearson. And because I promised, foolishly, nearly a decade ago that I would: Remember the Boohbahs!

I would also be foolish not to thank the tour guide at the National Gallery of London (who had no idea I was eavesdropping on the tour I did not pay for) for speaking of Vincent van Gogh with such passion that I cried in the middle of the museum. And to my uncle Freddy and aunt Christine, thank you for allowing me to crash your family vacation. London is where I was introduced to Vincent—where I discovered how easy it was to relate to an artist from over "a hundred bloody years ago"—so to that beautiful city: I thank you, too.

Last but not least, to Vincent van Gogh, for his beautiful art and his beautiful words. And to Jo van Gogh, for sharing these words with us. I needed them just as much as Fig did.